BREWING UP A STORM

RENEE JOINER

OSHUN
PUBLICATIONS
oshunpublications.com

JOIN MY
NEWSLETTER

GET UPDATES,
FREEBIES &
GIVEAWAYS

RENEEJOINERAUTHOR.COM/NEWSLETTER

Brewing Up A Storm © by Renee Joiner

Published by Oshun Publications

9 Old Kings Road STE. 123 #1038

Palm Coast, FL 32137

www.oshunpublications.com

Copyright © 2023 Renee Joiner

Disclaimer

Book design by Fantasia Cover Designs

www.fantasiacoverdesigns.com

ISBN 978-1-956319-74-3 (Paperback)

ISBN 978-1-956319-75-0 (Hardback)

ISBN 978-1-956319-73-6 (eBook)

ONE

Into the River

SEABROOK IS A SMALL, UNASSUMING TOWN HIDDEN DEEP IN the misty mainland of Florida. It's a charming mix of mossy cobblestone cottages, quaint shops, and an abundance of nature. The area itself is hugged by lush woods, with a small paved road that cuts through the west end, leading to a larger city about an hour's drive away. Seabrook is a town that houses people who are desirous of settling down to plant their roots and those who are content with a quiet provincial life. In spite of all these, however, it is a town that houses witches.

Of course, not every resident of Seabrook is a witch, especially since the number of witches in the world has dwindled in recent generations. People need help to know the reason why their relatives are dying. Some speculate that humanity is simply evolving beyond the need for magic. Others believe there are witches out there who kill their own kin. Whatever the reason may be, Seabrook is home to only a handful of witches in a population of 1,561 people.

One of these witches is Valeria Broussard, the owner

of a small perfume shop on the edge of town and master of elemental magic. When you look at her closely, you get the conviction that she was carved from the very elements that she draws her magic from. Her hair is a billowy cloud floating aimlessly about her head. Her skin is like the soil that her ancestors walked on for thousands of years, and when you look in her eyes, you see raging seas flecked with golden shores.

On this particular day, Valeria was deep in the woods surrounding Barton communing with nature… and collecting herbs and flowers for her perfumes. She kneeled down and pressed her palm flat against the drying mud while she closed her eyes and let the earth's energy flow through her. It felt like cool river water as it soared through her veins and acquainted itself with her desires.

Gelsemium sempervirens… Symphyotrichum elliottii. Asclepias tuberosa, she thought with focused intent.

She felt a slight tug in her chest, pulling her just off to the left and further into the woods. Her eyes opened slowly, and with a slight grin, she stood up and followed her intuition.

The tightly-woven canopy of leaves above her blocked most of the sky, so the streams of light that came through dappled everything in patches of warm golden sunlight. Valeria took care to step over the slick patches of moss and weave around the massive pine trees, which were still drying from the previous day's rain. If what her magic told her was right, then somewhere up ahead should be…

"Ah!" She proclaimed to nobody in particular. "Just as I thought!" She added.

Valeria lowered gently to a small damp which had on it an assortment of flowers. She sifted through them until she found one that looked like a sad drooping yellow bell, a few feathery pink stars, and a bundle of red beauties with spikes pointed toward the heavens. She picked them without disturbing the other flowers and carefully separated their petals from the stems.

Gelsemium sempervirens, Symphyotrichum elliottii, and Asclepias tuberosa, she thought to herself. Or in other words, their commonly known names are Carolina jessamine, Ezrat's aster, and Butterfly weed.

With her spoils in tow, Valeria returned to her perfume shop. She held the loose petals of the flowers in her left hand while their stems and leaves were placed in an ornate oak box that hung from her right hip. The petals were important for her business, but the rest of the flower parts needed to be stored appropriately for an entirely different purpose.

She reached her shop with ease after about 10 minutes of walking and unlocked the front door, making sure to flip over the sign in the window, which read: 'Open for Business.' The outside of the shop was nothing much to look at —it was a small cobblestone cottage like every other building in town, with a hanging wooden sign that read 'Elemental Essence.' It wasn't until you stepped inside the shop that the real magic happened, so to speak.

A wild assortment of glass vials and jars adorned several tables that spanned the rim of the room. Each container held some liquid or paste of varying size and color. If you were to get close enough, you could smell their contents without even having to open them— a whiff of spring rain, the aroma of bright flowers, an alluring scent of pine needles.

Of course, each of her perfumes had something reminiscent of nature—which only makes sense for an elemental witch. Now she was off to make even more of her signature scents. She sailed through the shop and tapped on her cell phone, which she had left on the front counter. The screen lit up with a display of the time 4:37 PM, but nothing else.

"Hmm…," she sighed in relief.

She usually heard from her husband, Kenji, every 10 minutes or so while working. Whether it was a text of a funny picture or a short call letting her know how much he missed her. When she did the math in her head, she realized that she had been out collecting materials for almost an hour. She glanced at a picture of the two of them hanging on the wall and pursed her lips.

He looked just as dashing in portrait form as in real life. He had deep brown eyes that reminded her of warm coffee on a cold winter's day and a cute curly pompadour that brought out the angles in his face perfectly. Where Valeria's skin was reminiscent of the earth's warm soil, Kenji's was more akin to the reddish-brown bark of an oak tree. Both tones were reminiscent of nature, which she believed was one of the many factors that drew her to him in the first place.

Maybe Kenji got lost in his most recent commission, which wasn't entirely unheard of. He worked in a small shop where he made wooden furniture out of the pine trees surrounding Barton—alongside his boss and two other men living there. It was a tough job for non-witches, but they all did fine.

There were a select few citizens of Barton who knew about the witches that resided there, and Kenji was one of them. Valeria was sure he would turn tail and run once he found out about her. Nonetheless, he had done nothing but go above and beyond to keep the secret of her coven ever since she told him about their existence. He had been her perfect husband and an amazing friend in her life.

Valeria shook the thought from her head as she stepped through the door to the back room and closed it behind her. He would reach out when he had the time to reach out. There is no reason to give it much thought or come up with any unnecessary concerns, she said to herself—especially when there was so much work to be done.

Three solid oak desks were resting perfectly in the middle of each wall. The one in front of her held all her materials in neat little boxes and jars. The one to the right was set up with perfumery equipment. The one to the left had a few odds and ends that most people wouldn't recognize. She would get to that one in a moment.

For now, she dumped the loose petals onto the first tabletop and sorted them into their respective jars. She left herself one clump of Ezra's aster petals to work with as she pulled a small container of solidified babassu oil and an empty yellow glass jar from the organized shelf in front of her.

She then scooped out enough babassu oil to fill the yellow jar most of the way and packed it in with a few presses of her thumb. Once the solidified oil was nice and level, she picked up a small blade and cut shallow slits into it. Then it was just a matter of pinching the loose petals into the slits, screwing the lid on tightly, and setting it aside to allow the scent of the flower petals to diffuse into the oil. That's the beauty of enfleurage—most of the work is just waiting for the components to work their magic and produce a beautiful scent in a few weeks.

Now that she was done, it was time for Valeria's final task for the day. She pulled the ornate box off its holder on her hip and set it down on the table to her left. She then unlatched the box and pulled out one of the stems with a tangle of thin brown roots dangling off the bottom. Turning it left and right, she decided the plant was sufficient and slid aside the rest of the box's components.

Next, she took out what looked like a regular mortar

and pestle. To any ordinary person, it would appear as a normal wooden bowl with a beautiful, but ultimately regular, onyx stick. When she picked up the pestle in her right hand, though, she could feel its immense power thrum through her flesh and into her soul. These were powerful apparatuses that only the strongest of witches could use properly, and Valeria was fortunate enough to count herself amongst the strong few.

She tossed the stem in the mortar and its roots and began grinding away in a rhythmic circle. She focused on each movement, placing her pestle in precise locations throughout the mortar. Her goal was to draw out the healing properties of the Carolina jessamine root just as she had drawn out the scents from countless other herbs and flowers. Of course, this process required an entirely different set of skills and demanded her utmost attention.

She thought back to the lack of notifications on her phone as she ground away, and a gnawing knot of unease formed in her stomach. She expected to have at least heard the vibration of a text notification or the sound of her unique ringtone from Kenji by now. Nonetheless, her phone remained silent throughout her rituals. What could have possibly preoccupied him to the degree that he would forget to send her a text as usual?

A plume of black smoke surged up from the mortar, and Valeria gasped as she stepped back to avoid it. The smoke rose in a perfectly straight tower all the way to the ceiling, then dissipated all at once when it came into contact with it. She leaned over to check the contents of the mortar and groaned. Just as she expected—she wasn't focused enough on the ritual and the whole thing combusted. Instead of a nice gray pulp and separated pink healing liquid, she was left with the charred remains of the plant.

Just then, a bell sounded from the front of the store, and Valeria saw the door open. She frowned and placed the pestle next to the mortar. She decided to suspend cleaning up her mess. She would have to go out again sometime after she closed the shop to pick some more Carolina jessamine. However, at this time, her customers demanded her attention. She wiped her hands on the front of her sweater, examined her face in a nearby mirror for signs of a singed eyebrow or charred hair, and stepped out of the back room.

Standing in the middle of the shop was her best friend, Landon—another non-witch of Barton who knew her secret. He was soaked from head to toe, and his bright crystalline eyes were wild as they shot around the shop and finally settled on her. She didn't know how she knew, but at that moment, she just… knew. Valeria sank to her knees as Landon approached her, and she squeezed her eyes shut as if they would stop those damning words from coming out of his mouth.

"It's Kenji," he gasped, wiping river water from his face. "He's dead!" He announced.

TWO

A Storm Rages

VALERIA'S EYES FLUTTERED OPEN WITH GREAT EFFORT. HER gaze slid weakly left and right, carefully analyzing the scene around her. When she realized everything was the same as before, she let her eyes slide shut with a soft groan.

She was in bed, just like she had been almost every day for the past week. If she reached her hand out to the other side of the bed, she would be met with a cold empty space. If she were to prick her ears for the sounds of Kenji cooking breakfast in the kitchen, she would hear only her heartbeat thundering in her ears.

Therefore, she simply closed her eyes. She waited for the agonizing pain to wash over her just like they did every day since she got the news that her amazing husband had died. It took a moment, but then there it was, as sure as the tide, as sharp as broken glass, and as potent as poison—the foulest concoction that the heart could ever conjure for the human body.

She could still feel the ache in her legs from sprinting out into the street and down toward the river where Landon said they found Kenji. When she flexed her right hand, she could feel the sting of the rash, now healing, from when she tripped and scraped her palms on the street.

She got there at the right time, as a few townspeople pulled his body to the shore. One of them was babbling incessantly off to the side while he was saying something about how they saw a man walk into the river. She strode past him and knelt next to the corpse, but she didn't need to look into those soaked features to know that it was her husband. She could feel a ragged, gaping hole somewhere deep in her core. It was the same feeling that had bothered her earlier in her shop—the feeling of a part of her soul, her very being, dying.

The sound of a jaunty ringtone broke through Valeria's fugue state. She reached over and blindly patted around on her nightstand, using her fingertips to search for the shape of her cell phone. When she finally found it, she withdrew her arm and tucked the phone close to her face so she wouldn't strain to see the screen. She opened her eyes, and her heart stopped when she read the name that popped out on the screen. It was Landon.

Her mind immediately flashed back to that day in her shop. His eyes practically glowed with panicked mania, with the sound of his shuddering breaths from sprinting all the way to her. She gritted her teeth and slid her finger over the screen to answer the call.

"Hey," she croaked out weakly before clearing her throat.

"Hey, Vale, how ya holding up?" His voice was careful without being condescending, and she could detect a note of genuine concern.

It wasn't Landon's fault that Kenji died. He had no part to play in her husband's supposed suicide. Of course, she didn't expect her best friend of 16 years to patronize her, especially after everything they had been through together. Landon was her rock when her parents died in a ghastly car crash. He supported her when she had to move in with her grandmother, Gayle, and he stayed by her side when she told him she was a witch. He was even the best man at her and Kenji's...

"I'm alive."

"Are you?"

Valeria groaned as she pushed herself to a sitting position, threw off the covers, and slid off her bed.

"There ya go," Landon's encouraging voice piped up from the phone. "You should get yourself some water while you're up."

She frowned as she padded across the cold floor and into her kitchen. He was right, of course. Landon was always right. She'd been having difficulty taking care of herself this past week, and some hydration would definitely do her some good.

"You know what else would do you some good?" His voice crackled from the speaker once again, almost as if he were reading her mind.

"I Don't, but I'm willing to bet you will tell me."

"I think it would do you good to get out of the house. You've been cooped up there all week, and I know how easy it is for you to spiral into your little pit when... things like this happen."

"Mhm!" She pulled a cup down from the cupboard and filled it halfway with water from the sink. When the cool liquid touched her lips, she realized just how thirsty she was, and she immediately drank the rest of the water. She filled the cup up once more as Landon went on.

"Maybe you should try going back to work today. You don't have to open the shop, but you could at least get yourself busy with your little concoctions and potions."

Valeria thought back to the charred remains of the Carolina jessamine plant and frowned even harder when she realized the mess was still there, waiting for her to clean it up.

"And once you're done with that, maybe you should visit Gayle."

She froze in place, the full cup of water resting at her lips as Landon's words sunk deep into her. She hadn't even thought of her grandmother this past week though she typically visited her every other day for lunch or just to catch up. When Valeria thought about it deeply, she realized that Gayle was probably worried about her. That was enough to kick her into gear. She placed the cup back down on the counter with a nod.

"You're right. I just need to get out of the house for a while, clear my head, and get some fresh air. Kenji... Kenji would want that for me."

"Exactly, do it for him. I'll swing by tomorrow with some groceries for you. In the meantime, just do your best and keep on going."

With that, Landon hung up and left Valeria to her own devices. It took some effort for her to change out of the same pajamas she had been wearing for the past week and shower, but once she toweled off and put on a fresh pair of clothes, she could tell that she felt a little bit lighter. Even though it wasn't anywhere close to being 'healed' or 'okay,' she felt fairly better.

Valeria took off toward her shop, making a conscious effort to keep her head down and avoid the gazes of those around her. It was a small town, and word inevitably spread fast. She managed to make it to Elemental Essence in one piece, and for a brief moment, she felt she could make it through the day. Then the smell of burned foliage assaulted her nostrils, and her eyes immediately spiked with tears.

It was all she could do to robotically move through her duties and complete them to the best of her ability. She scraped the charred remains of the Carolina jessamine into a nearby compost bin. She then wiped the mortar and pestle down with an anointed rag. She briefly considered going out and fetching another flower to re-do the process. With all the things going on within her inner self, she knew she would never be able to give the ritual the necessary attention.

Instead, she moved through her inventory, checking on the progress of her recent perfumes while setting out the appropriate jars and vials for the ones that would be finished soon. When she finished with the inventory, she wiped down all the counters and tables in the shop and swept the floors. Soon enough, she was left in the middle of a pristine and spotless shop… with nothing else to do. She thrummed her fingers against her hip for a brief moment before abruptly dropping her broom in the middle of the floor.

Alright. Time to see Gayle, she thought to herself.

Valeria quickly closed the shop and took off toward her grandmother's house on the opposite side of town. She kept her head down again, but she could still sense that storm clouds were beginning to form in the sky above her. Their dormant electricity tingled the nerves at the very ends of her fingertips. This was positive as it filled her with enough energy to make it to her grandmother's doorstep.

The door opened only a few moments after she had knocked, and Gayle's pleasantly surprised face poked through the opening.

"Oh, Valeria! Come in, my dear, please come in," Gayle said.

The older woman stepped back and opened the door further for her granddaughter. Gayle shuffled toward the back of the house while Valeria closed the door behind them. She sat down on the couch and took off her shoes. Her grandmother's house always smelled vaguely of some type of baked good, and today it smelled like…

"I'm so glad you decided to visit," Gayle's voice floated out of the kitchen. "I just finished up a fresh batch of poppyseed bagels. I used this new garlic butter from the store down the street. Oh, you're going to love it!"

Valeria stepped through the kitchen to find a tray of steaming bagels cooling off on a wire rack and saw her distant cousin, Sadie, standing indifferently off to the side. Sadie moved in when Gayle first fell ill about four years ago, and she has been taking care of her ever since. Sadie was another powerful witch, but instead of the elements, her domain of power was blood magic.

As for Gayle herself… Valeria could never quite pinpoint what type of magic she had mastery over. It was not that her grandmother was ever secretive about her magic. It was just that it was always too complicated for Valeria to get a solid grip on. She'd seen Gayle perform incantations and mix potions, but she never understood what they were for.

"Hi, Sadie," Valeria forced a small smile as she sat down on the kitchen table.

"Hello, Valeria," her cousin responded in a clear and even voice with no emotion whatsoever. "I'm sorry to hear about what happened to Kenji."

Valeria's heart clenched in her chest, and for a brief moment, it felt as if she couldn't breathe. As typical of Sadie, she always tended to speak whatever was on her mind and would do so without considering the feelings of anybody in the room. After a moment passed, Valeria drew a sharp breath and bit down her lower lip.

"Oh, of course," Gayle added with much more sympathy, "words can't even begin to describe how sorry I am. I wanted to visit you at some point, but as you know, my sickness...."

Her grandmother trailed off weakly, but Valeria didn't need her to finish the sentence anyways.

"It's okay, grandmom. I understand. It was time for me to get out of the house anyway, so I figured I would drop by for a visit."

"Of course, it was time," Sadie piped up heartlessly. "It isn't becoming of a witch of your stature to wallow in self-pity, after all."

"Sadie," Gayle cut in sharply, but it was too late. Valeria was already on her feet, her eyes wide open and her entire body trembling. It took everything in her power not to collapse in a weeping pile on her grandmother's kitchen floor, but that power wouldn't hold up for much longer.

"I have to go," she managed to squeak out pitifully before lurching away from the table. She could barely hear Gayle reprimanding her cousin as she sailed out the front door toward her own house. When she got home, it felt as if only a few moments had passed before she threw herself into bed and yanked the covers over her head.

A quick sob escaped her before she broke down entirely. Her entire body was wracked with the force of her torrential cries, and each broken wail ripped from her throat seemed to shake the house itself. She realized after a few moments that she had subconsciously grabbed a nearby hanging picture of Kenji. Valeria was grasping it so tightly to her chest that the corners were digging into her skin.

Right on cue, a crack of thunder sounded overhead, and a downpour of ferocious rain immediately followed. Valeria allowed the fierceness of nature to pierce her soul as she mourned the loss of her other half. This was how things had gone every day for the past week. A vicious storm popped out of nowhere every night, and at least a few lightning strikes hit the same area of the river where Kenji had died.

How did Valeria know that? Well, her powers were always amplified under violent conditions of nature, whether it was storms or hurricanes, earthquakes, or tornadoes. She felt in her very being the precise location of each lightning strike, and although she didn't know what it meant, she knew it meant something. It was something she was too worn out to figure out at that moment.

She kissed the picture of her late husband through gasping sobs and allowed herself to fall into an uneasy sleep.

THREE

Misgivings

VALERIA SIGHED AND AGAIN OPENED HER EYES TO AN EMPTY bedroom. Soft yellow light filtered through her window and illuminated dust motes that spun and whirled gracefully like ballerinas. She blinked once before blowing a sharp gust of wind in their direction. The dust motes' balletic dance turned into a frenzied panic as they jolted left and right to escape the violent gale. Still, Valeria's elemental magic was too strong of a force for their frail structures.

Hmm, she thought aimlessly as she pursed her lips. "I guess it's been a while since I've dusted around here."

That thought was interrupted momentarily by a knock at her front door. Valeria groaned and pulled the covers over her head, hoping beyond hope that whoever it was would leave her alone. At this time, it was noon, and she had long given up the idea of going to work for the day. All she wanted to do was lie down in solitude and wallow in her misery.

Unfortunately, her visitor knocked once more on the door, insisting that she rise from her despondency and interact with the outside world. Valeria slid out of bed and briefly considered changing out of her wrinkled T-shirt and food-stained shorts but then decided against it. If she was being forced out of her new comfort zone, she would do so on her own terms.

She opened the door to find Landon standing on her front step with a soft smile. He had a bag full of food in one hand and a broom in the other, which he held in front of him. Valeria took the broom from his hand and stared at it blankly before looking back at her friend.

"What! Is this supposed to be my new mode of transportation or something?"

Landon screwed his mouth into a confused frown.

"What do you... oh! Oh, okay, yeah, I get it, haha. 'Cause, you're a witch. Witches fly around on brooms."

"Witches don't—Landon, have you ever seen me 'fly' on a broom before?"

"Not that I can recall, but then again, you could have wiped my memory or something."

Valeria looked down at the broom once more and shook her head.

"What are you doing here? And why did you give me a broom?"

Landon stepped past her and into the house, using his heel to kick the door closed behind him. He left Valeria standing confused at the threshold of her home while he moved toward the kitchen.

"I called yesterday and said I was bringing some groceries, remember? The market just got some fresh zucchini this morning. I thought about making you some sort of vegetable pasta dish."

"And the broom?" She asked once more, holding the cleaning tool out in front of her in emphasis.

"I cook; you clean." He responded simply.

Valeria thought back to the dust motes in her bedroom and shook her head.

"I don't want to."

"I know you don't," Landon shrugged as he pulled a pot down from a high cabinet, "but you have to. It might not make you feel better, but you will have a clean space to wallow in."

Valeria sighed before touching the bristles of the broom down to the floor. As much as she wanted to go back to bed and cry, something deep inside her knew that Landon was right. She eventually had to take steps toward living her life again, and cleaning her home was an easy first step. Therefore, the two started working and got themselves busy with their tasks in silence.

"You know," Valeria eventually piped up, "I have a right to wallow."

"Of course you do," Landon replied with complete sincerity. "You just lost your husband tragically, Vale. Nobody expects you to be okay."

She thought back to her interaction with Sadie the day before and winced. She knew her cousin could be blunt and to the point, but what she said was just downright cruel. Valeria could feel the same pain from their conversation bubbling up again, and her thoughts turned to the events of the last night—running home, hiding from the world under her covers, the storm…

"I think I'm going back to the river."

Landon dropped a plate that he was cleaning, and it clattered noisily against the floor as he turned to look at her in shock.

"What? Why on earth would you want to do that?"

Valeria held his hands out to get him to listen to her.

"Hold on, there's a reason. Something has been

happening ever since Kenji died, and I just think that if I went there, I could…"

"Vale, I don't think that's a good idea."

"But each night…"

"Vale," Landon repeated with a groan as he rubbed the back of his neck. "What do you think you're going to accomplish by going there? I'll tell you what's going to happen, even though you're not going to like hearing it."

"Landon, if you would just…"

"You're going to that spot where they found Kenji's body, and you would break down all over again. Not even the most powerful magic in the world could bring him back, and you're not going to gain any closure by torturing yourself."

Those words brought her up short as she pressed her lips together. She hadn't thought about that when she decided that she would go to the river. There was a real chance she could tear open the barely-scabbed-over wound again and prolong her healing. Then she remembered why she even wanted to go to the river first and shook her head.

"No, you don't understand; it's not for Kenji. Or rather, it is for Kenji…, or it has the potential to be for Kenji?"

Landon picked the dropped plate up from the floor and stared at her, puzzled.

"What are you talking about? Did something happen?"

Valeria threw her hands out and scoffed in exasperation.

"That's just the thing! I don't know if something happened. I just have this feeling, and there was this strange thing with Kenji just a few days before he died."

Landon's eyes went wide, but he kept his lips sealed as she went on.

"I didn't mention it at the time because I didn't really

give it much thought. He kept saying that there was something he wanted to tell me, but every time he tried, he would forget what it was. I just figured that maybe he was tired or stressed out from work, but now that I think about it… I don't know."

"Do you have any idea about the nature of what he wanted to tell you? Whether it was good or bad?"

Valeria closed her eyes and recalled those few days before her husband's death. She could vividly see the frustration in his eyes as he struggled to remember whatever he wanted to tell her. She could almost hear his exasperated groan as he gave up on recalling it.

"I couldn't tell whether it was something good or bad, but I remember feeling distinct that it was urgent. He desperately wanted to tell me and kept bringing it up over those few days."

"Maybe he just forgot something he wanted to tell you, and that's all there is to it."

"But that's not all, Landon. We've been getting these electrical storms every night since Kenji died, right? They seem to just conjure up out of nowhere, and every night lightning strikes the river in the same spot where his body was found."

That was enough to get her friend's full attention. Landon turned off the stove and moved the pan to the side before he turned to face her.

"I'm assuming you know that because of the whole witchy intuition thing, right?"

Valeria nodded, and Landon mimicked her nod thoughtfully.

"That's strange, especially since lightning isn't supposed to strike the same spot twice. Let alone numerous times…."

His hand went to his chin as he thought over what she

said. After a few moments, he dropped his hand and sighed in relief.

"Maybe there is something to all of this, or maybe it's all just some horrible coincidence. At the end of the day, I just can't piece it together."

"Me neither," Valeria responded dejectedly as she moved to sit at her kitchen table. "I just know that Kenji was struggling to tell me something a few days before he died, and every night since that happened, we have been getting these terrible storms. Landon joined her at the table and put a comforting hand on her shoulder.

"Hey, storms aren't so bad. They water crops, and they give us an excuse to stay inside, and..."

"No," she interrupted, "they're not awful in that sense. There's just something... off about these storms. I don't really know how to explain it. This foul pain sparks the air when they come on, and it's entirely separate from the pain I feel. It's so sharp and acute that I swear I can feel it physically prick my skin."

Landon took in this new information and frowned.

"So, what does all of it mean then?"

She met her friend's gaze briefly before sighing and looking down.

"I don't know, Landon. I really don't know," she replied pitifully

FOUR

You're A Doll

VALERIA WAS BUSY CLEANING THE DISHES FROM LUNCH when her phone rang. She placed the plate she was working on off to the side and dried her hands on a towel while it rang two more times. Finally, she stepped over to where her phone was on the kitchen table and glanced at the screen. When she read the name on the screen, she froze in place.

Greta, Kenji's mother, was the name that popped up.

Valeria gasped as she fell to her knees. She hadn't been able to face his family since that first phone call, the one where she let his parents know that their son was dead. She could still hear the animalistic howl ripped out of his mother and the odd choking sound that his father made in the background. If anyone knew even a fraction of the pain that she was going through, it was them.

The phone let out another ring, fell silent for a moment, and then rang again. Valeria leaned against the nearest table leg and hugged it tightly. For a brief moment, she hid there motionless, as if Kenji's mother was in the room with her. The phone rang once more, and she rose with a sigh. There was no point in hiding. She was going to have to talk to her eventually. At this time, Valeria resolved to answer the call and held the phone up to her ear.

"Greta?"

"Hi, dear," the older woman on the other end of the line answered.

With just those two words, Valeria could feel the low spirits of her mother-in-law. Her normally soft voice was barely audible. Even then, Valeria could still hear the stark agony in her wavering tones. Those words were floundering hands lost at sea, desperately grasping for anything to keep her afloat. Valeria drew in a deep breath before responding.

"It's good to hear your voice. I would have called you sooner. It's just...."

It's just what? she thought desperately. It's just that I've been struggling to find a reason to wake up every day for the past week. It's just that Kenji is dead, and nothing makes sense anymore. It's just that even now, you remind me of him, and that makes it hard to think or breathe.

"I understand," Greta replied simply.

And, of course, she did. Who else would know what Valeria was going through more than Greta? She lost her son, just as Valeria had lost her husband and best friend. She was probably going through the same things her daughter-in-law was going through. In fact, she must have had to muster an obscene amount of strength just to make this phone call in the first place.

"Anyways," she went on, "I was just calling to let you know that we have everything set up for the memorial service tomorrow."

Valeria couldn't help but flinch when she said that. She had been so wrapped up in her pain that she completely forgot about the memorial. Kenji's parents were holding it at their house on the north side of town, and they sent her the information just the other day.

"Of course."

"I expect the whole thing to take at least an hour or two. It's really just the townspeople that are attending, so...."

She trailed off, and Valeria got the impression that just those few sentences had taken a lot out of her. She gritted her teeth and tried her hardest to speak steadily.

"I'll be there. Thank you so much for calling and letting me know. I'll see you tomorrow."

"Yes. Tomorrow."

The call ended, leaving Valeria just as drained as she presumed her mother-in-law was. She wanted to just crawl back into bed for the rest of the day. If anything, she felt like she deserved a break after such an intense conversation, even if it only lasted a few sentences.

Unfortunately, she had plans for the day.

Gayle had apparently contracted a cold overnight and ended up in the hospital. It wasn't too drastic, but even a minor illness would usually hit her pretty hard due to her compromised immune system. The doctors gave her some fluids through an IV, and she has just been taking it easy since then. When Valeria got the call, Gayle was in the hospital. She promised she would visit her as soon as she could. She fetched a small cloth bag and placed a fresh loaf of bread, a water bottle, and a few vials containing potions for pain inside. Her grandmother had always harbored a distaste for manufactured painkillers. Valeria had a hunch that she was in more pain than she let on over the phone. She tried to scoop her phone up from the table and lock the doors before heading out.

It wasn't hard to find her grandmother when she arrived at the hospital, which was a small town. The nurse at the front desk led her to the room where Gayle was admitted, and when she opened the door, she was surprised to find Sadie standing next to Gayle's bed.

"Oh, hey," Valeria said as the nurse closed the door behind her. "What are you doing here?"

"I'm the one who brought Gayle in, of course," her cousin responded coolly.

"Well, I just figured that maybe you would be too busy to stay, though."

Sadie raised her eyebrows at that.

"What would make you think that?"

"I don't know," Valeria moved to her grandmother's bedside and began sorting through her bag. "I just feel like you're usually busy whenever I see you. In fact, you're probably the busiest witch that I've ever met in my life."

"I have duties to attend to," she responded.

"Hi, Valeria," Gayle cut in as she smiled at her. Valeria smiled softly as she pulled one of the vials out and shook it back and forth.

"I brought something to make you feel better. I've been trying out a few recipes here and there, so you have a few options. This one is derived from the root of the Gelsemium sempervirens, which is poisonous in its natural form. However, when I use a separating spell, it actually…"

"She doesn't need any of that," Sadie interrupted. "I've already made her a salve to control her temperature and a potion to remedy the pain."

"Oh."

Valeria started to tuck her potions away when Gayle shot her arm out to stop her.

"Wait!"

Valeria froze in place and stared at her grandmother with a quizzical expression. However, Gayle's burst of energy didn't last long, as her arm fell almost immediately back to her side.

"I would still love to try out your potions," the old woman said as emphatically as she could. "These effects will wear off soon enough, plus I'm curious to see what you have come up with this time."

That made Valeria feel a little bit better, but there was still something strange in her grandmother's reaction. Maybe she really was in more pain than she let on.

"The one with the Gelsemium sempervirens essence is supposed to help with pain brought on by sickness, which is why I think you should try it first. Otherwise, there is one for nerve pain and another for muscle pain," Valeria explained.

"Hmm… tell me more about that first one. Gelsemium sempervirens, you said?"

Valeria perked up slightly at Gayle's interest, and she jumped right back into her explanation.

"The root of Carolina jessamine is poisonous, but I discovered that using a certain spell on its components separates it into the physical husk of the root and the liquid inside the root. As it turns out, the liquid contains healing properties in its purest form. So once I separated it from the root, I ran the liquid through a purifier, and it gave me this."

She held up a small vial containing a viscous pink liquid. When she turned it on its side, she could see tiny crystals floating aimlessly around inside of it. The crystals refracted the light from the fluorescent bulbs ahead. They bent it into wondrous rainbows that painted Gayle's awe-stricken face.

"This will cure pain from any sickness," the old woman started saying as she stared into the vial's contents. "Is it possible that… it could cure sickness itself?"

Valeria understood the implications of what she was asking. Although her grandmother never admitted it, she knew she was terrified of death. Gayle had done everything in her power (and others) to cure herself since she first learned of her diagnosis. But even the strongest witch couldn't reverse the fate of death.

"I'm not sure," Valeria responded carefully. "You will be the first witch to try this potion, so I suppose you will be the first to find out whether it does or not."

Gayle took the vial from her granddaughter and slipped it into her pocket with a shaky hand.

"Thank you, my child." She smiled lovingly from her bed and patted the top of Valeria's hand. "You truly are a doll."

Valeria immediately recoiled as if she had been slapped. She could feel her heart begin to race, and her lungs restricted to the point that her breaths came out in sharp wheezes. Valeria took one step back, then another, before collapsing weakly to her knees.

"Doll... you're a doll." That's exactly what Kenji used to say to her any time she would do something sweet for him or any time he would just stare at her with endless love in his eyes. He would tell her that she was a doll, and then she would make some dumb joke about how they were like Barbie and Ken. Gayle must have picked it up from him, but when did she...

"Valeria?" Gayle sat up in alarm as Sadie rushed to her cousin's side. Valeria tried to tell them that she was okay, but a pained cry slipped out when she opened her mouth. That was all it took for her to start bawling right there and then on the hospital floor.

"What's the matter with you?" Sadie asked sharply as she supported Valeria's weight, stopping her from crumbling in on herself.

"It's…she…why would you?" Valeria struggled to find the words through gasping sobs, but Gayle immediately picked up on her intention.

"Oh, sweetheart," she sighed sympathetically, "was it something I said? Did it remind you of Kenji?"

It was all Valeria could do to nod as Sadie grumbled and groaned by her side. She felt her grandmother's hand on her shoulder, and when she looked up, she saw the old woman gazing deeply into her eyes.

"You say the word, Valeria, and I'll make this all go away for you."

She stared at Gayle's blurred form for a moment before wiping the tears from her eyes.

"What do you mean?" She asked with a confused frown. "What are you making go away?"

"The pain, of course," Gayle responded simply.

Valeria could feel Sadie stiffen at her side, which was never a good sign. If Sadie didn't like what Gayle was referring to, then it must be something serious. Valeria did her best to steel herself as she returned her grandmother's gaze. She knew that the answer to her next question could very well break her, but she also knew that she needed to hear what Gayle had to say.

"How? How can you make this pain go away?

"We can erase all memories of Kenji," she replied simply. "It's an ancient, complicated spell, but if completed correctly, it will be like he never existed. Other than the occasional tip-of-my-tongue feeling, you will go on and live your life in peace and—"

"No!" Valeria cried out as she jumped to her feet. "How could you even suggest such a thing, Gayle? Kenji was everything to me, and even though his death has caused the worst pain I have ever felt, it wouldn't be remedied by just erasing his existence. That would be just too cruel."

Gayle's eyes darkened, and for a moment, it was almost as if she were an entirely different person. Valeria could feel her immense power practically radiate from her. She was no longer a frail grandmother confined to bed rest but a powerful witch who had domain over nearly all. Then the moment passed, and Gayle pressed her lips together wistfully.

"You're right, my dear. What was I thinking?"

FIVE

The Memorial

VALERIA SAT ON THE EDGE OF HER BED, PICKING ANXIOUSLY
at her nails. She had trouble sleeping the previous night,
but it wasn't entirely the storm's fault this time. She
couldn't stop thinking about her grandmother's odd reaction when she refused to have her memories of Kenji
erased. It was almost as if she took personal offense to it,
although Valeria couldn't even begin to fathom why such a
thing could have caused any insult.

Maybe Gayle genuinely thought that Valeria would be
better off that way. Maybe she figured that she knew best,
and her granddaughter was being foolish by not letting her
help with the pain she was going through. Now that
sounded more like the tough, loving, witchy head of the
family that Valeria knew and loved. But that dark look in
her eyes...

She shook her head and looked over at the black dress
on the bed next to her. Whatever was wrong with Gayle
would have to wait. She had been sitting in the exact same
spot for over an hour. It was finally time for her to get
ready for Kenji's memorial. She fingered the material of

the soft dress aimlessly and allowed her thoughts to drift away again.

And once more, she found her thoughts turning to the same thing they had turned to since the demise of her husband, the charm. More specifically, the protective charm that Valeria had given Kenji the day they got married. On the outside, it looked like a regular leather necklace with a small clear quartz hanging, but they both knew the immense power of the simple piece of jewelry.

Valeria performed the entire ritual to create the protective charm herself. She hunted, killed, and skinned the deer whose flesh she turned into leather. The smallest bone in its body, and the deer's heart, were then ground up into a paste and smeared onto pure quartz while she recited a spell nearly as old as time itself.

Valeria's mouth turned down in a frown as she thought about the ritual she had performed that day. She had created many protective charms for other witches, so she was no stranger to the incantations and methods required. Nonetheless, she was continually haunted by the thought that she must have messed up something in the process.

If Kenji's protective charm worked the way it was supposed to, it should have protected him from drowning in the first place. Even if he did kill himself, which Valeria still didn't believe was true, the charm would have forced him to tell her about his intentions. That's the whole point of a protective charm in the first place. To protect the person that it is bound to from anything and everything.

Valeria knew that she should be getting ready for the memorial, but she felt compelled by some unknown force to double-check her book of spells. If there was anything that could put her mind at ease, it was the clothbound compendium that every witch of considerable power possessed. The words on those weathered pages would prove whether she had completed the ritual correctly.

Valeria got up and moved toward her front room. She kept her own book of spells hidden underneath a loose floorboard, just in case any non-witch visitors decided to snoop around. She knelt down and conjured a small gust of wind to lift the loose board. She set it quietly off to the side while she scooped the worn book up from its hiding place.

Conjuration Compendium

The book was bound in deep green cloth, and as she flipped the pages, she could feel how soft they were from frequent use. She used the compendium for everything, from her own personal potions to incantations for her work. Magic has its benefits outside the world of magic, and Valeria could hardly go a day without utilizing something from this book.

It didn't take long for her to find the portion of the book that dealt with healing and protection. She flipped to the proper page and moved her finger along the weathered paper, reciting the words in her head as she read them. She went over the spell again and again after that.

It was just as she thought. She had read the incantation perfectly that day. There was not a single word or syllable out of place, which shouldn't have come as a surprise, but still ended up breaking Valeria's heart. If she had found some sort of mistake or realized that she had misread a portion of the spell, then at least she could blame Kenji's death on something other than cruel fate.

So that was it, then. Kenji's death would remain mysterious, and Valeria finally had to get dressed in her mourning gown and attend his memorial. She felt helpless as she slipped the long dress over her head and pulled it down over her body. It was becoming increasingly apparent with each passing second that there was nothing Valeria could do about her predicament. Her husband was dead, and life would have to go on. The earlier she came to terms with this reality, the better for her.

She checked herself in the mirror one last time before leaving. On the surface, she looked exactly the way she always did, but she knew her own reflection better than that. The life behind her eyes was simply... gone. What were once roiling seas were now tame, dead waters. She held herself up high with the pride of her heritage, but there was no strength behind her posture.

How was she expected to go on?

Valeria scoffed as she turned away from the mirror. She would just have to do what she'd been doing for the past week and keep going. She would have to keep finding motivation that wasn't there so she could continue waking up, continue going to work and continue living. So, she put one foot in front of the other, not even knowing why she bothered doing so and made her way to the memorial.

She stopped short just as she walked up to the front of Kenji's parents' house. Just like her, the place looked the same as it always did; but she knew that. Also, like her, there was nothing but pain inside. She and Kenji had come to this house to have dinner with his parents a week before he passed on, but she couldn't bear to think about that right now.

She opened the door without knocking and stepped into a room full of people dressed all in black. Countless eyes turned on her with pity, and she immediately felt the need to duck her head and hide. Nobody tells you that you practically turn into a zoo animal when a loved one dies, and sometimes you wish you could sink into the ground. People can stare at you all they want under the guise of sympathy, and you just have to deal with it.

A pair of hands saved her from the mob as they grabbed her gently by the arms and led her into a side room. When Valeria turned around, she was met with a concerned-looking Landon, who immediately hugged her. She let him hold her for a moment before pulling back and looking up at him in confusion.

"Hey, what are you doing?"

"Saving you from a really uncomfortable situation," he replied with a soft smile. "It's mostly just the townspeople out there, and I get the distinct feeling that they would have flocked to you if they were given a chance."

"Oh, thank you."

She returned his smile for a brief moment before she remembered why she was even there in the first place.

"Where are…"

"Kenji's parents are in the backyard touching up a few things before the memorial begins. It should start here in a few minutes, so if you want, we can just sneak around to the back and get seated before anyone notices."

Valeria nodded gratefully as he took her hand and led her through the empty parts of the house. It was strange for her to be in this house without her living and dead husband. His burial was taken care of the day after he died by her family and his, so this whole service was just for closure.

She stepped out into the backyard just as Kenji's mother was wrapping up her preparations. A few dozen white folding chairs were set up in neat rows, and at the head of it, all was a beautiful arch of flowers and foliage. Valeria could sense that every bit of nature had been collected from the surrounding forest town, and she felt a surge of pride in the effort Kenji's mother put in for him.

She was just setting out the last chair when they stepped outside, and she looked up at them with the same dead look that Valeria had seen in the mirror earlier. She immediately felt guilty for not calling or visiting her earlier, but then she realized that Kenji's mother probably felt the same need for isolation that she felt.

"Hi, Valeria," the older woman said in a voice as dead as her eyes. "Feel free to take your seat here upfront. I'll call the others out in just a moment."

Valeria nodded and led Landon to the first two seats right in front of the floral arch. She waited for Kenji's mother to finish her final preparations, but instead, she just stood there, taking deep breaths. She understood then that she was preparing herself rather than her surroundings for what was about to come.

After a minute, she moved to open the back door. Soon enough, people were filtering outside and taking whatever open seats they could find. Kenji's father sat on the far-left side of the row she was on, and Valeria was pained to see that he looked just as anguished as his wife. She knew this would be a sad affair, but after seeing his face, she was suddenly unsure if she would be able to hold herself together.

Kenji's mother opened the memorial by talking a little about her son's life and who he was. None of this was news to the attendees, but they all understood that it was cathartic to just talk out loud about those we lost. When it was his father's turn, he recalled a few humorous stories from Kenji's childhood. And then it was Valeria's turn.

The mother, the father, and the spouse were expected to speak at the deceased's memorial. Valeria knew this and couldn't come up with the energy to write a eulogy for her late husband. She tried a couple of times, and she really did. Nonetheless, she inevitably ended up breaking down in a sobbing mess and giving up on the entire matter.

So she would have to improvise. She walked up to the

front and stood amidst the beautiful arch built out of the very essence of her magic. She could feel the energy of the plucked flowers and leaves gathering around her and flowing through her veins, giving her the energy she needed to speak up.

She opened her heart and let its contents come flowing out. She talked about how she and Kenji met and how quickly they fell for each other. She regaled the audience with a few of their adventures together. She ended the eulogy by claiming how unfair all of it was. She was met with supportive 'awws' from the crowd as she took her seat, and when she brought her hand to her cheek, she was surprised to find that it was dry.

She did it. While talking about him in-depth, she managed to keep herself together at the house Kenji grew up in, surrounded by his friends and family. The rest of the memorial went off without a hitch. When everybody moved inside for food and congregation, Valeria snuck out and headed home before anybody could notice. Sure, she had a small Landony today, but it was meaningless in the grand scheme of things at the end of the day. As she walked off in solitude, one thought kept repeating itself.

How unfair.

SIX

A Wolf in Sheep's Clothing

THAT NIGHT, BLAZING LIGHTNING CRACKED FEROCIOUSLY overhead, bringing thunder that practically split the skies. Valeria had never experienced such a violent storm before. Nonetheless, she couldn't bring herself to be frightened by it. Maybe it was because the power of the storm surged through her, or perhaps it was because she felt as though that night's storm only confirmed her suspicions.

The fact that these storms occurred every night—with multiple lightning strikes hitting the exact spot where Kenji died—was too dubious. She had this nagging thought every night for the past week that these storms were trying to tell her something; she just didn't know what it was. She drew in a deep breath and wondered once again if she should...

Crack!

The sky opened with another volley of thunder, enough to send Valeria jumping out of bed with determination. If she had any doubts before, that just confirmed things for her. She decided to go to the river that night. She didn't know how, but she just knew that going to the spot where her husband died was somehow going to answer her questions. Or, at the very least, bring her some form of closure.

Ignoring the faint sound of Landon's warnings in her mind, Valeria pulled on her raincoat and sailed out the door. This was the most alive she had felt in what seemed like forever. She bounded down the wet street and spread her fingers, allowing as many raindrops as possible to hit her skin. She could feel the power of precipitation flow through her as if she were made from the same water, which was enough to propel her even faster toward her destination.

She arrived at the river just as a lightning bolt came down from the sky. She watched as it arced toward the bank, then, at the last second, bent to hit a peculiar spot in the water. She stood in awe as two more lightning strikes hit the same spot in only a minute. She knew it—something supernatural was going on there!

Just then, she heard a voice calling out from a distance. She paused and tilted her head, straining to hear anything over the pounding rain and booming thunder. A moment passed before she heard the cry again... at the same spot where the lighting was striking! She stared incredulously at the water, but she could tell nobody was there, even in the soft moonlight.

Without thinking, she took a step forward and then another one. The crying voice was becoming a little clearer, but she still couldn't discern what it was saying. She continued slowly until she stood right at the river's bank. As her foot touched the boundary between soil and the water, the voice cried out again.

"Help! Please, somebody, anybody, help me!"

Valeria couldn't discern the age or gender of the voice she heard. It was almost like an amalgamation of old and young, male and female voices. The ambiguity frightened her, but she managed to push through her fear as she waded into the river toward the spot where the lighting was striking.

She used her powers to make the river flow around her rather than push up against her. When she felt the crackle of lightning in the air, she redirected it to hit the bank rather than the water. As she moved forward, the strange voice grew louder and more frantic until it stopped altogether. She looked back toward the bank and realized she had made it to the spot where Kenji had died.

She stretched her arms out and turned her palms to face the sky. Her eyes slid closed as she focused intently on her surroundings, using her intuition to see what the environment had to tell her. She stayed like that for a few moments, but nothing came to her. Her eyes spiked with unshed tears as she turned her face to the stormy sky.

"What is it?!" She cried out to the heavens. "What did you bring me here for? What is it you want me to know?!"

Suddenly she felt something small yet sturdy fall into her right hand as if it were dropped from the sky. Her eyes flew open in surprise as she looked down at the object. It was difficult to see it at first. Then another strike of lightning illuminated her surroundings, and her heart froze.

It was Kenji's protective charm.

Just then, a gust of wind kicked around her, and she could hear the faint ominous whispers. The voices blended together so she could hardly hear what they were saying, but she picked up portents of doom and warnings of treachery. She shook her head as their words came faster and faster, struggling to glean some sort of meaning from them. Then she picked up two words so eerily clear it was almost as if they were spoken directly to her.

Gayle Henry

Valeria was so taken aback by the name that she lost her grip on her powers for a moment. The surging river pushed up against her and threatened to drag her under, but she managed to force it back as she made her way back to the shore. Oddly enough, the second she touched dry dirt, the storm above her seemed to dissipate immediately, leaving the skies clear and calm in only moments.

Valeria's head was reeling as she stumbled away from the river. She couldn't make sense of anything. Why wasn't Kenji's protective charm with him, and how did it fall from the sky like that? Whose voices were whispering to her in the wind, and why did they bring up her grandmother's name? She didn't have the answers, but she could feel a knot of unease forming in her stomach. She had to figure out what all of this meant.

She took a step in the direction of her home when an unexpected wave of apprehension washed over her. For some reason, the house that had protected her from the outside world this past week suddenly seemed unsafe. She knew this was ridiculous, but for some reason, she couldn't shake the feeling that she shouldn't go home just yet. So instead, she turned and headed toward her shop, where she decided to study Kenji's protective charm further.

When she stepped through the front door of her shop, she was met with a stale emptiness and the smell of hundreds of perfumes. Nobody had been there since she made Gayle's pain management potions a few days ago. The thought of her grandmother's name brought on a strange tension at the back of her brain, but she shook it off as she moved into the back room and got to work.

She set the protective charm down and took out a magnifying glass from her toolkit. She barely had to pass over the quartz charm to see the issue. The quartz had held its form just fine over the years, but when she looked closely, she could see dark mist clouding the clear crystal.

Valeria felt a sharp jolt in her heart when she realized that the charm might have been tampered with, but a simple clouding mist wasn't enough to prove it. She searched thoroughly through her drawers and containers until she found small rectangular sheets of cloth paper piled in a neat little stack. She withdrew a single sheet and a nearby needle made from pure iron.

She pricked her finger with the needle and immediately pressed the cloth sheet against it, allowing her blood to soak into the fibers. As she did so, she recited an incantation that she had memorized from heart, imbuing the cloth with searching intention. She then wiped a section of the crystal and gasped at the results.

Weathered brown hands could be seen as an apparition of the deepest parts of the quartz. The face above them was shrouded by the dark mist, but Valeria watched as the crystal reflected the most recent ritual that was performed on it. It should have shown her the protection ritual she performed on it many years ago, but the hands in the reflection...

Valeria dropped the protective charm as she stumbled backward and fell to the floor. The quartz bounced harmlessly off the hardwood, but she now knew just how much power that small crystal really held. The evidence she uncovered was undeniable—somebody had tampered with Kenji's protective charm before he died.

She thought back to the old-looking hands in the reflection, and her grandmother's name whispered in the wind. Bile rose in her throat as she considered the possibility that Gayle might have had something to do with Kenji's death, but it didn't make any sense! She never even hinted that she harbored any murderous intent toward her grandmother. In fact, Valeria was positive that her loving grandmother wasn't capable of such evil.

But the more she thought about it, the more things started to fall uncomfortably into place. Witnesses said that Kenji had just walked into the river, almost sounding like he was being controlled by some outside force—some magical force. Then, Gayle's name whispered almost accusingly in the wind, and those storms...

Suddenly, Valeria realized something—the storms! They occurred every night, and lightning struck the exact spot where Kenji died multiple times per night. She didn't know why it didn't happen to her earlier, but she realized what they meant now with a sickening twist in her stomach.

Kenji's spirit was trapped in the atmosphere, and he was trying to warn her about his untimely demise.

Just then, her cell phone rang harshly from her pocket, and she withdrew it to find that Gayle was calling. Valeria almost tossed the phone away from her in fear. She didn't want to talk to her grandmother, especially when she uncovered her murderous and evil plot. On the other hand, she didn't want to arouse Gayle's suspicions when there was still so much to figure out about all of this, so she resolved to answer the phone.

"Hello?" She could barely keep her voice from wavering.

"Hey, Valeria," her grandmother's voice responded in an almost bored tone. "I'm finally out of the hospital, no thanks to the medicine of the mundane, of course. Your potion has been working splendidly. I just wanted to thank you for taking the time to make such a thing for me."

"Of course."

"Anyways," Gayle continued, "I'll be having lunch tomorrow with Sadie, and I wanted to know if you would tag along. I want to thank you properly, and you know there are no better thanks than a grandmother's love in the form of food!"

Her worn voice rang out in laughter, but Valeria's voice was caught in her throat. She couldn't bear the possibility of facing her grandmother after everything she had just found out about her. Moreover, the chance of arousing suspicions tickled the back of her mind, so she gritted her teeth and nodded.

"Absolutely, Gayle. I would love to join you for lunch tomorrow."

And just like that, the date with the murderer was set.

SEVEN

The Culprit

VALERIA WALKED TOWARD HER GRANDMOTHER'S HOUSE with her head in the clouds—or rather, with her head clouded. The storm never returned after it dissipated last night, so she had a decent night's rest for the first time in a while. She figured that she would wake up feeling more rested. However, she only found herself more exhausted than usual as her thoughts spun with the events of the previous day.

The voice that whispered Gayle's name kept playing over and over at the back of her head. Gayle Henry, Gayle Henry, the voice repeated. It said the name as both an accusation and a warning. Almost as if she should keep a wary eye on her grandmother. She still couldn't fathom that Gayle had something to do with this, but then she thought about the state of Kenji's quartz when she brought it back to her shop.

She could see it just as clearly in her mind's eye as she did that night: weathered brown hands reaching out and potentially tampering with the crystal. Then there was that dark mist which only proved that the crystal was tampered with. It was all almost too much. Valeria stopped in the middle of the street and drew deep breaths.

She didn't want to suspect that her grandmother had a part to play in her husband's death. As a matter of fact, she wished with all her being that this was all some sort of misunderstanding. Of course, if her grandmother actually murdered Kenji, all the wishing in the world couldn't stand up against incriminating evidence. At the moment, everything pointed toward Gayle as the prime suspect who tampered with the crystal. Then again, these were only suspicions, nothing truly concrete. That was why she accepted the date with Gayle in the first place, so she could observe her closely to see if she had given anything away.

Valeria steeled her nerves and went briskly down the street, making it to her grandmother's house in 10 minutes. The front door was already cracked open, so she tried to slip through it as quietly as possible without causing it to squeak.

She leaned forward on the balls of her feet and padded softly down the hallway, keeping an ear out for the sound of conversation. She could hear Gayle murmuring something in the kitchen up ahead, presumably to Sadie, so she made her way forward. As she crept closer and closer, she could hear soft words more clearly.

"I just think we shouldn't have done it that way," Gayle muttered adamantly. "Look, we've made things that much harder for ourselves."

Valeria peeked around the corner and nearly jumped out of her skin. Sadie was standing just off to the right where she couldn't see, and when her head rounded the corner, she found herself face-to-face with her accusatory glare. Valeria stumbled into the room out of shock. Gayle was sitting casually at the kitchen table, staring at her surprisingly.

"My goodness, Valeria!" She laughed exuberantly as she raised her hand to her heart. "I didn't hear you come in, dear. I'm so sorry. What on earth were you doing over there?"

"Listening in on conversations that she isn't a part of," her cousin answered.

"I..." Valeria struggled for words as she looked back and forth between Gayle and Sadie. "I just... wanted to know what the latest gossip was."

"Oh, it's nothing like that at all," her grandmother answered with a light hand wave. "I was simply telling your cousin that we should have baked the bread my way instead of trying this new thing... uh, what did you call it, Sadie? Confetti?"

"Confit," her cousin answered promptly. "I wanted to add confit garlic, but..."

"It just ended up burning on top of the bread," Gayle said. "So now, instead of cutting the slices fresh, we have to wait for the loaf to cool down before picking off the garlic."

"Oh."

Of course, that made sense, but now that Valeria was suspicious of Gayle, she couldn't help but wonder if she had just made up the lie on the spot. She moved to the kitchen table and sat next to her grandmother, looking at the neat array of bowls and plates spread across the table. There were deviled eggs, cubed fresh fruit, and a row of steaming zucchini boats and croquettes for the main dish.

Valeria found that for the first time in a week, she was actually starving, and without thinking, she reached out to grab a croquette and move it onto a nearby plate. She suddenly realized why she was here in the first place and froze with her hand hovering just over the food. She could feel Sadie's intense gaze boring into the back of her head as she slowly withdrew her hand and tucked it back by her side.

"What's the matter, sweetheart?" Gayle asked endearingly. "Aren't you hungry? I can tell that you haven't been eating that well recently. That's why I cooked all of your favorites."

She was definitely right about that. Everything on the table looked mouth-wateringly delicious to Valeria. Nonetheless, that whisper in the wind started playing in the back of her mind again. In it, she could hear undertones of treachery, of danger. What if Gayle knew Valeria was suspicious of her and poisoned the food? She forced a small smile and shrugged.

"I thought I was hungry, but I just don't know if I can eat right now."

If she was still in the clear, Valeria knew that she had to commit an innocent act to avoid arousing Gayle's suspicions. She searched deep in her heart, in the tucked away crevices that still horrifically ached for her dead husband, and looked back up at her grandmother with tears in her eyes.

"I'm so sorry, Gayle," she whimpered. "I know you put a lot of effort into this lunch, but I…"

"Hey there, it's okay." Her grandmother reached over and covered Valeria's hand with her own. It took everything in her power not to flinch away, and she had to mask her discomfort by covering her face and pretending to cry into her hand. Gayle patted her hand a few times before withdrawing her own, and suddenly it was like Valeria could breathe again. This might be harder than she thought.

Sadie moved to join them at the table and promptly initiated a conversation with Gayle, ignoring Valeria entirely. She took the opportunity to observe the two women as they discussed empty things such as the garden's health and whether or not they would go to the neighbor's baby shower the following week. To avoid being suspicious, she grabbed a few deviled eggs and took small, almost pained bites.

After a few minutes, Valeria actually started doubting her suspicions. Gayle didn't look like a bloodthirsty murderer—she cupped a mug of warm coffee between hands that shook intermittently. When she laughed a little too hard, her voice would warble for a moment before tapering off. If anything, Valeria thought she looked a bit… weak. Her sickness must really be taking a toll on her.

Sadie looked the same way that she always did. Cold and detached. When Valeria was growing up, she always thought of her older cousin as a machine wrapped in human skin. She kept herself calm and collected despite being a powerful blood witch. Her face never gave away what she was thinking about. Not even now.

Valeria grew increasingly uncomfortable as her suspicions and reality continued to clash. Gayle was very good at hiding ulterior motives. However, it was also possible that she had misunderstood the situation entirely. Maybe the voice in the wind whispered Gayle's name because she had tried to save Kenji, and maybe those old hands in the reflection of the crystal belonged to someone else.

"Excuse me." Valeria piped up in a small voice.

She pushed herself back from the table, and her grandmother looked up at her with concern in her eyes.

"You're leaving already? Are you sure you don't want to pack anything along with you?"

"No, Gayle, thank you."

Valeria took off before her grandmother or her cousin could protest. Sitting across from the woman who had raised her since she was ten years old, it didn't feel right, subconsciously accusing her of murder. On the other hand, something about the lunch atmosphere was just unbearable. Even though Valeria couldn't pinpoint the source of her discomfort, she knew she had to get out of there.

She thought over that word 'atmosphere' again and looked at the sky. A few lazy clouds ambled about through a stark blue sky, all of which was illuminated by a bright orange sun—the clearest weather that Barton had experienced all week. She thought about the possibility of her husband's soul being trapped in the atmosphere, unable to move on to a peaceful afterlife, and her heart shattered.

Her intuition took over as she withdrew into herself. She suddenly found herself in the same vulnerable state she was trapped in for the first few days after Kenji's death. The memories of their life together raced through her mind, and each time she saw his bright smile in perfect detail, she felt the barely-scabbed-over wounds rip open once more.

When she eventually came, she realized that she was standing at the entrance of Barton Cemetery—the place where both her parents and Kenji were buried. She looked around herself in confusion, wondering why her intuition brought her to the one place that would only make her pain worse. This was apparently her soul's desire, so she braced herself as she moved through the graveyard toward the plot that held her loved ones.

It only took a minute for her to reach her family's plot. There were three ornate obsidian headstones lined side by side neatly that Valeria had carved all by herself. There was also a lush growth of flowers and clovers spread over the graves, which she also created by herself. She came here once a month to tend to the growth of her parents' flowers, and it was only natural for her to come here the night after Kenji's burial to add his own flowers to the bunch.

She knelt between her father and Kenji's graves and pressed her palm against the loose soil. Reaching deep down into the earth with her powers, she drew nutrients and water into the flowers and watched them grow more vibrant with each passing second. When she was satisfied with her work, she went to withdraw her hand, but something inside her kept her grounded.

She pushed down with her powers once again and sensed the rectangular shape of the empty coffin six feet beneath her. Of course, Kenji was never actually buried here. She and a few other witches gave him a proper burial amongst the forest's foliage, so his body could give back to the earth that provided for them. It was a painful affair, but there was a sense of rightness to it that she knew Kenji would have appreciated.

She tilted her head up once more, but this time, instead of gazing into the sky, she simply closed her eyes and allowed the warm sun to wash over her. Though her powers were enormous, they weren't enough to extend into the atmosphere and sense the presence of her husband. She wanted nothing more than to feel him one more time and let him know he wasn't alone.

"I am going to help you, Kenji," she said with determination. "I swear on the very foundation of my powers. I'll free you, my love."

EIGHT

A Friend in Need

VALERIA OPENED HER EYES TO AN UNNERVING SENSATION. She slowly sat up in bed and put her hand over her chest, trying to discern why she felt so off. Her heart thumped away steadily, and her breath came easily to her, but her body felt almost sluggish. It was almost as if she...

Oh.

She realized right away what it was. The storm hadn't returned since that night at the river, so she had been getting some decent sleep over the past few days. The strange feeling was her being well-rested for the first time in a while. She stretched her arms out and wiggled her toes, relishing the feeling of wakefulness for a brief moment.

Then reality set in, and Valeria felt her heart sink. For a second there, she almost forgot that she was caught up in some sort of awful murder mystery involving her dead husband, where her own grandmother was the prime suspect. She didn't wake up with the image of Kenji's tampered crystal in her head or the faint sound of the whispers in the wind. She was just a normal woman waking up on any normal day.

Except she wasn't a normal woman; she was a witch—a witch who needed to find out what had happened to her husband so she could free his soul and send him to the peaceful afterlife that he deserved. She shook off the impending dread that she had grown accustomed to over the past couple of days as she dressed for the day.

Valeria had a daunting task ahead of her, but she knew what had to be done if she would go ahead with her plan. She pulled on a worn pair of blue jeans and a gray T-shirt, trying to look as inconspicuous as possible. She would have to go out today and didn't want to draw any unnecessary attention to herself.

But first, she needed an accomplice.

As that thought passed through her mind, she heard two sharp knocks at the door, followed by a pause and three more sharp knocks. She moved into her front room and stepped to the front door as quietly as possible. Her power stretched forth as it felt the air outside and conformed around the shape on the other side of the door, a lanky man standing at exactly six feet and three inches.

Valeria opened the door to find Landon standing on the front stoop with a concerned expression. She wasted no time waving him inside. He followed her sense of urgency as he practically leaped over the threshold to her home. In the same movement, Valeria pushed the door shut and swung around to face him with a sigh of relief.

"Landon, you have no idea how happy I am to see you."

"As I am to see you," he responded cautiously. "But first, I would really like to know what this is all about. The sneaking around and knocking codes…"

"I'll explain everything, I promise," Valeria cut him off.

"But we can't talk here. I want you to take a walk with me. We're going to this place in the forest where I am collecting some materials for the shop. You can't talk the entire way there, and I'll let you know when it's safe to speak again. Okay?"

Landon opened his mouth to answer, then pursed his lips and nodded. Valeria nodded gratefully back at him before leading him quickly outside. She stayed close to his side with their arms interlocked, but this was only so she could set the pace for them. They would look like two people arm-in-arm out for a casual stroll through town to anybody watching—all the more inconspicuous.

She led him to her shop, where they walked through the front door, but then she immediately banked right and took him out of the side door and off to the forest. Again, if anybody were watching, it would look like they were simply shopping around for perfumes. She kept quiet all the way until she reached her spot, which was about a 15-minute walk outside of town.

"Hold on," she muttered as she held up a finger. She used her powers to reach out around her, trying to sense anybody who might have followed them. Her field of magic extended outward a hundred feet, then two hundred, but as far as she could discern, it was just the two of them. Her shoulders sank in relief as she gave Landon small thumbs up.

"Alright, we're free to talk now."

"Free to talk about what?" he threw his hands up in exasperation. "What on earth is going on, Vale? What could be so important that we have to take such evasive measures just to talk about it?"

Valeria opened her mouth again but then closed it after a moment. She wasn't quite sure how to go about this. How could she look her best friend in the eye and knowingly involve him in whatever insidious plot was going on? What if she was putting him in danger by doing this? She stared at his concerned eyes and decided she would just have to take the risk. She needed an ally in all of this, and he was probably the only person she trusted absolutely and unequivocally.

"I believe that Gayle had something to do with Kenji's death."

Landon's eyes went blank with confusion. He frowned, shook his head, then frowned even harder. She could practically see the wheels turning in his head as he struggled to comprehend what she had just told him. Finally, after almost an entire minute, he responded with one word.

"What?!"

"I know," she immediately held her hands up to calm him down. "I know how that sounds. It's ridiculous to even think about, but…"

"Of course, it's ridiculous to think about, Valeria! You just said that Gayle, your grandmother and the woman who has taken care of you since you were ten years old, had a part to play in Kenji's suicide?"

"But it wasn't suicide!" she cried out. "You and I know that Kenji was never the type to take his own life, especially in the way he did. Plus, when I went down to the river the other night I…"

"Vale," Landon groaned as he pinched the bridge of his nose. "I told you not to go there."

"I know you did, and I tried not to, but something about this just wasn't adding up. So I went to where he died, and this voice was crying out to me from the river. It was calling for help, Landon."

Her friend looked at her warily while he rubbed the stubble on his chin.

"Was it… Kenji calling for help?"

"No, it didn't sound like him. It didn't sound like anyone, actually. It was just an ambiguous voice that sounded in danger."

Landon nodded as he followed along and motioned for her to continue.

"Okay, so I followed the voice into the river, and when I reached the spot where Kenji died, it just stopped. I waited a few moments, but nothing happened, and then suddenly, Kenji's protective charm fell from the sky."

"Woah!" Landon breathed in awe.

"Yeah, but it was all wrong. I took it back to my shop to inspect it some more, and I found that it had been tampered with. There was this odd dark mist clouding it, and when I performed a ritual, I saw a pair of old-looking hands manipulating it with magic in its reflection."

"Well, that doesn't mean it was Gayle," Landon said. "Many old people live in Barton, specifically a number of old witches. It could have been any one of them."

Valeria thought back to the faint amalgamation of voices whispering in the wind and the name they spoke in warning her. She couldn't help but shudder.

"There was this other voice," she started. "Well, it was more like many voices all speaking through each other. They whispered a single name to me through a gust of wind. Gayle Henry."

Landon's face shifted from uncertain to grave in a matter of seconds. It was clear that he was taking her seriously despite his own personal feelings and thoughts about Valeria's grandmother. She was sure that this was just as hard for him as it was for her considering the fact that he always viewed Gayle as a motherly figure too.

"So you're saying that some voice spoke Gayle's name to you, and you discovered evidence of tampering with the quartz in Kenji's protective charm and an image of old-looking hands performing a spell on it."

"That's right."

Landon continued to rub the stubble on his chin, thoughtful for a moment more before shrugging wearily.

"It doesn't sound good. I can tell you that much. But the evidence you found just isn't concrete enough for a conviction."

"I know," she responded with a resolute nod. "That's why I didn't tell you when this happened a few days ago. At first, I couldn't believe it, but I also couldn't. I needed to dig more, so I joined Gayle and Sadie for lunch and studied her up close."

"That was a pretty dangerous thing for you to do, especially considering the possibility that Gayle might be a murderer."

"I know," she repeated, "but don't worry, nothing happened. Nonetheless, I think I need to lay low from here on out. I no longer feel comfortable in her physical presence, so I'll have to stop visiting her."

"But how are you going to gather more evidence if you're not even going to be near her? If that's your plan, then finding out what happened to Kenji dead ends here. You're stuck with whispers only you heard and a pair of hands belonging to some old person."

"I'm not stuck because that's not my plan at all. I'll find out what happened to Kenji and bring whoever tampered with his protective charm to justice."

"So I ask again. How?"

Valeria smiled wryly and looked back in the direction of the town.

"I know someone who might be able to help."

NINE

Fortune Favors

Valeria had Landon stay over at her place that night so she could watch over him. If Gayle did have something to do with her husband's death, then who's to say that she wouldn't go after her best friend next? It didn't matter whether she believed Gayle was capable of such things. It still gave her peace of mind to have him in her line of sight. Moreover, it was nice that she didn't have to wake up to an empty home again.

"So, what's the plan for today?" Landon asked when she emerged from her room the following day. He was already dressed and cooking breakfast for the two of them, seemingly geared up and ready to go.

"We're going to visit a friend of mine. She owns a shop just on the inside of town," Valeria responded.

"A friend of yours who also owns a shop in Barton?" Landon cocked an eyebrow at her in confusion. "Why haven't I met her yet? I know practically everybody in this town."

Valeria couldn't help but chuckle at that, despite the seriousness of their conversation.

"You have met her. You just can't remember it."

"Why wouldn't I be able to…oh. She's another witch, isn't she?"

Valeria nodded in confirmation, which turned Landon's mouth into a frown.

"I don't like people fiddling with my memories, you know."

"I know, but it wasn't without good reason. Trust me."

Landon slid two over-easy eggs onto a plate with buttered toast and sat it down in front of her. He sat across from her as she dug into her food and stared at her with gravely piercing eyes.

"Vale, if I'm going to be jumping into this with you, then I'll need to know everything. Who is this woman we're visiting, and what are we hoping to achieve by seeing her?"

Valeria chewed thoughtfully as she thought about how to answer him. After a few moments, she swallowed her food and cleared her throat.

"Alright, so here's the skinny of it: My friend is a very powerful witch specializing in seeing magic. She can see into the past and the future and control what others around her see. That's why you don't remember meeting her—every time you met her, she caused you to see someone else in her place."

"Oh, okay, that makes sense. But why even bother with making people see her as someone else in the first place?"

Ah, yes. Here is where the real heart of the matter lies.

"As I mentioned, she's a very powerful witch—definitely more powerful than me and almost as powerful as Gayle. She has spent practically her whole life being recruited into dark arts and black magic by other witches who wish to use her. So eventually, she just went into hiding. She allows those she trusts to view her for who she really is and cloaks her identity from everybody else."

"So that's why I never 'met' her then, huh? I'm not deemed trustworthy enough?"

"It's not that you're not trustworthy, Landon," Valeria responded with a roll of her eyes. "You're just mundane, that's all."

"Mundane. Right? So, we'll meet up with this powerful witch at her shop to do… what, exactly?"

"I'm not exactly sure yet. My friend's power of sight isn't limited to humans; she can also see things through objects. I thought we could take the quartz from the charm to her and see if she can see anything from it."

"Wow," Landon breathed. "Can she really do that?"

"Again, I'm not exactly sure." Valeria frowned and pushed the rest of her food away. "You have to understand that this is a unique situation; it's not entirely unheard of for a witch to turn on her coven, but it is a rare act. To top it all off, whoever tampered with Kenji's protective charm did a good job covering their tracks, so… who knows."

"And how are we to know that we can trust her? I mean, think about it—we're working off the theory that your grandmother had something to do with Kenji's death. If you can't trust the woman who raised you, how could you trust someone who hides from her own kind?"

It's an understandable concern on his part, thought Valeria, but the answer only ended up twisting her heart.

"She was one of the few witches that helped me put Kenji's body on the earth."

"Oh." Landon pursed his lips as he thought for a moment. "Who were the others?"

"They were two witches from her coven who had come to Barton for the sole purpose of the burial. They're long gone now, and besides, I don't know them well enough to trust them with something like this."

And with that said, Valeria pushed herself back from the table.

"I understand things aren't looking too good for us, Landon. The number of people we can trust is abysmal, and the small amount of evidence we have is even more so. Our path ahead is fraught with danger, and if we're somehow wrong about this, then that means disownment for me and, most likely, a memory wiped for you. Still…"

"Still?" her friend prompted.

"Still, I promised Kenji I would do this for him." She stood up and lifted her head high. "If you want to back out of this, I wouldn't judge you. I can make another protective charm just for you and…"

Landon leaped up and put a hand out to stop her.

"No need for any of that, Vale. I'm with you on this through and through. Let's visit this witch and see what she says about all of this."

The two took off on another forcibly casual walk in town. Valeria was on edge the entire time and kept stretching her powers out to see if anybody was lurking around the corner or down a nearby alleyway. Once again, she couldn't detect any lurking assailant—but that didn't necessarily mean that there weren't any out there.

Despite her fears, they made it to the shop unscathed. It was vaguely reminiscent of her own shop outside of town—a small, unassuming cobblestone cottage with broad windows showcasing the goods sold inside. Instead of a hanging wooden placard, this shop had an ornate iron sign nailed above the front door with the words' Fortune Favors' carved in gold.

That wasn't the only difference, though. Valeria cupped her hands to peer through the windows and was immediately greeted with an odd assortment of tarot cards, gems, and other mystical paraphernalia. There were voodoo dolls hanging from one portion of the ceiling and shrunken heads dangling in another. A few people milled aimlessly about inside, taking in the fantastical and weird at their own pace.

This was the genius establishment that was 'Fortune Favors'—a tourist attraction and shop of oddities that boasted fortune-telling services to those willing to pay. In other words, it was a method of hiding in plain sight for a witch on the run. Her friend set up the shop in this small and unassuming town many years ago, and so far, her ruse had worked out perfectly in her favor.

Speaking of her friend, she could spy on the woman coming from a side room with a customer. The customer was a middle-aged man with a shaky smile and tears in his eyes, and he was being led out by a woman who appeared to be as old as time. Her eyes were glossed over with milky cataracts, and her skin repeatedly folded on itself with countless wrinkles that hinted at a well-lived life.

The old woman was saying something to the customer when she paused and turned her blind eyes to the window. Valeria quirked her mouth up in a half smile, and the old woman immediately reciprocated the gesture with a beaming grin of her own. She waved a welcoming hand to Valeria as she led the customer to the front counter, presumably to pay for his real brush with the ethereal.

Valeria took Landon's arm and led him inside the shop. The two meandered around the store while the old woman was busy wrapping up her transaction, picking up a few oddities here and there to inspect them closely. Valeria passed her hand over a deep purple amethyst and took a moment to feel the power of its strength thrumming out from it.

Right there was the magnificent ruse of the shop. Every bit of magical paraphernalia was magical in the truest sense. Any regular person walking through Fortune Favors would see plain cards painted with tarot symbols and regular old minerals that had crystallized over time. However, any witch worth her salt would know the true story of those items.

It was really genius in every way. The old woman could hide in plain sight, and nobody would be any wiser. If a witch were seeking her out, they would pass right over her ridiculous little shop, making it out to be some sort of money-grabbing scam by a mundane shop owner. And if, for some reason, they were a little bit more suspicious and decided to enter the shop, she could merely use her powers to hide from them and play innocent.

"How nice of you to visit me, young child," The old woman welcomed Valeria playfully.

The creaky voice came from just over her right shoulder, practically dripping with playfulness. Valeria couldn't help but grin softly at her friend's absurd pet name for her.

"Oh please, Quinn, I'm two years older than you."

"And I've been a shop owner for five more years than you have, so I win."

Valeria placed the amethyst on the table and turned to face her friend. She knew that the haggard old woman in front of her was just a guise, but it didn't change the fact that it was a damned good one. She could hardly see her friend underneath the plentiful folds of flesh, even when she focused with all of her power.

Valeria motioned toward the shop's back room, indicating that she needed to speak privately with her friend. Quinn's eyes immediately sharpened as she picked up on the gravity of her request. The old woman wasted no time turning on her heels and clapping once loudly to get the rest of the customers' attention.

"Apologies, my lovely patrons," she cried in a wavering voice, "but I must close up the shop early today! I am an elderly woman, after all, and I can only go on for so long. So good day to you all, and good fortune!"

Quinn glided into the back room, not even waiting to see if the customers were leaving her shop. Fortunately, the shoppers filed out one by one until it was just the three of them left in the shop. Landon stepped over to join Valeria and ventured into the back room of Fortune Favors.

They came upon Quinn, shaking herself in the center of the room like a wet dog. Instead of water, it was glamor that flicked off of her in minuscule droplets and accumulated into a colorful puddle on the ground. After a few moments, a stunningly beautiful young woman, who turned her ember eyes on them at once, stood in her place.

"What brings you to my humble shop today, Valeria? I'll be frank. I wasn't expecting to see you out of the house so soon. Whatever it is must be very important."

She reached a hand out to Valeria, who shook her head in return.

"Trust me, Quinn. It would be better to tell you what happened rather than show you."

The young woman turned her fiery gaze on Landon, who shifted uncomfortably on his feet.

"Very important indeed," she continued as if she hadn't heard her friend, "seeing as you've conscripted the services of a mundane."

Valeria took a deep breath and figured it would be better to get her concerns out there.

"My grandmother, Gayle Henry, had something to do with Kenji's death."

Quinn stared blankly at her for a few moments. Her

eyes glazed over as she attempted to understand what exactly Valeria had just told her, and it was all she could do to just blink slowly as the words worked their way through her brain. After what felt like an eternity, Quinn returned Valeria's sigh with a deep groan as her eyes darkened to a deep orange burn.

"Tell me everything."

TEN

Look Inside

VALERIA PULLED UP A STOOL AND SAT DOWN WHILE LANDON continued to stand awkwardly by her side. She pulled out the tampered quartz from her pocket and held it to Quinn.

"I found this—Kenji's protective charm—while I was in the river the other night. It fell out of the sky, and I think some spiritual force delivered it to me."

"Wait, what?" Quinn shot both hands in front of her, signaling Valeria to slow down. "You were in the river the other night? Doing what, exactly? And what are you talking about? His charm fell from the sky?"

"You might want to start from the beginning." Landon chimed in, cringing almost imperceptibly when Quinn turned her sharp gaze on him.

"And what exactly is his role in all of this? Don't get me wrong. I trust you just as much as any other witch in my coven, but I don't shed my glamor for anybody."

"Landon knows everything I am about to tell you, and I trust him just as much as I trust...."

Valeria bit down on her lower lip and trailed off. She was about to say that she trusted him just as much as she trusted Gayle, but after all, she was here because of Gayle. The trust she had for her now was shaky. Once again, the reality of her situation came crashing down on her as her eyes began to well with tears. Quinn immediately softened and pulled up a stool so she could sit across from her.

"If you're not going to let me see what happened, then you must tell me. Your friend here is right—just start from the beginning, then go from there."

Valeria drew a deep breath to steady herself, then launched into her story.

"So these freak lightning storms started popping up immediately after Kenji died, right?"

"Of course," Quinn responded. "They were happening every night for a while there. I didn't think to connect them to Kenji's death, though."

"Well, I did, and as it turns out, I was right to believe they were connected. One night I went out to the river where Kenji died…"

"Against my advice," Landon cut in before shrinking away from Quinn's glare.

"Yes, against his advice." Valeria pressed on. "But like I said, I was right that the two were connected. I went to where he died and immediately heard a voice calling out from the river."

"Oh, Valeria, you gotta be careful about those. That could have been a forced hallucination, or even worse, a trap…"

"I know," she cut her off exasperatedly, "just listen to what I have to say, please."

Quinn motioned as if she were sealing her lips, so Valeria continued.

"I moved to the middle of the river, but right when I got to the place the voice was coming from, it stopped.

Then Kenji's protective charm fell right into my hand, almost as if it were placed there intentionally by someone."

Quinn's eyes went wide with interest, but she kept her mouth shut.

"After that, this unnatural gust of wind picked up, and I could hear countless voices whispering over and through each other. I couldn't pick up what they were saying until two words came through as clear as day: Gayle Henry. Then the storm just… stopped. As if its entire purpose was to lead me to those clues."

Valeria turned the ruined crystal over in her fingers before holding it out to her friend.

"I took the quartz back to my shop to inspect it and discovered that it had been tampered with. There's this dark mist clouding the center of it, and when I used an uncover spell, I could see that the most recent ritual performed on it was done by a pair of hands that looked just like Gayle's."

She could still see the dark shrouding mist inside the quartz. It undulated slowly as if it had a life of its own and was even trapped inside the fractures of the crystal; it practically dripped with malicious intent. Quinn took the quartz from her and held it tightly between her pointer finger and thumb.

"Woah," she breathed. "Yeah, this has definitely been tampered with. Even holding it feels wrong… what kind of dark magic is this?"

Hearing those words made Valeria's stomach turn. She knew that the quartz was defunct, but she had no idea just how wicked the magic instilled in it was. Dark magic was among the most powerful of the insidious arts. It could only be used by the most powerful of witches. It didn't make her feel any better to know that Gayle's powers were undoubtedly strong enough to wield such magic.

"What can you see in it?" Valeria asked uneasily.

"Nothing other than the pair of hands you mentioned. The ritual that was performed on it is blocking my sight, so I'll have to perform a ritual of my own if I'm going to be able to dive any deeper. I'll be able to see the past from Kenji's point of view since he had such a close connection with this protective charm, so hopefully, that will help shed some light on all of this."

She flicked two fingers as if she were warding off a fly, and suddenly, all the lights in the room went out. She could hear her friend shuffling around and picking up a few things for a moment before a soft glow illuminated the room. The light source came from a set of three pure diamonds that Quinn used only for the most energetic of rituals, and in her right hand was a cloth similar to the one Valeria used in her own ritual.

Quinn sat on the floor in the middle of the room, perfectly centered in the triangulated diamonds. She wrapped the quartz entirely in the cloth and held it to her core, focusing intently. She then whispered an incantation under her breath that Valeria had never heard before. When her words stopped, the quartz and Quinn's eyes lit up with shimmering purple light.

"What can you see now?" Valeria whispered.

"There's a room," her friend responded in a voice that was flat yet layered at the same time. She could hear Quinn's throaty tone while she could hear another bassy voice underneath it. When she focused intently on it, she realized that the voice sounded similar to Kenji's.

"What's in the room? Describe it to me."

"I can see... a dark wooden table. It's a long oval shape, flat, and low to the ground. One of the legs in the back is partially broken, and there's a book underneath it holding the rest of the table level. The name on the book's spine is "Dead of the…' something."

"In the Dead of the Night," Landon mumbled. He turned his eyes intensely on Valeria, whose horror-stricken gaze reflected his own.

"There's a bookshelf behind the table," Quinn continued. "It's large and takes up the entire back wall. Most of the books are magical in nature, but a small section in the bottom right holds children's stories. To the left of the cabinet is a solid oak cabinet with many locks, and to the right is a green cloth sofa. The sofa looks old and has a few patches here and there."

Valeria could feel Landon stiffen next to her, and she immediately understood why. Quinn was describing every last detail of Gayle's spell room. Her grandmother cuddled up with her on that same green couch when she was younger and read her children's stories from the bookshelf. One time when she was showing off a spell to a 12-year-old Landon, she accidentally damaged one of the legs of her table. She replaced it with a copy of In the Dead of Night that was about the same size.

"There's something on the table," Quinn reached out in front of her, most likely mimicking Kenji's actions in the memory. She pinched something between her fingers, lifted it up to her face, and furrowed her eyebrows in confusion.

"What is it?" Valeria could barely manage to ask.

"Hair… wrapped in twine," her glowing eyes flicked from the imaginary item in her fingers to the non-existent table in front of her. "There's also a vial of what looks like blood and another vial filled with a few drops of a clear sparkling liquid. I can see a book turned open to a specific page, and some of the words are circled in red ink."

"What does the page say?" Landon jumped in. "What words are circled?"

Quinn leaned forward as she tried to read the words on the page, but then the light in her eyes flickered. She shook her head and tried focusing on the book again, but her eyes flickered once more.

"It's starting to blur…" her layered voice was frustrated and apprehensive. "I can't see clearly—this memory has been tampered with."

Valeria froze in place at those words. She thought back to how scatterbrained Kenji seemed in those last few days of his life, how he was desirous of telling her something but couldn't remember what it was. Did Gayle wipe a portion of Kenji's memory? She knew that her grandmother was capable of such a feat, especially after she offered a memory-wiping spell when she visited her at the hospital.

"What can I do to help?" she cried out desperately.

"You also… have a bond to Kenji," Quinn strained to get out. "Lend me… your connection."

Valeria thrust her hand into Quinn's, and the light in her eyes immediately steadied. The stress seemed to lift off her as she peered again into the past.

"I can see now. There is a book on the table, and it's opened to a page detailing an incantation for…."

Quinn jerked back in shock. She squinted her eyes at the words only she could see, and her mouth dropped open in disbelief.

"Oh my God… it's a channeling incantation for a spell that dates back to the beginning of the world. This is ancient magic that not many witches in the modern world know how to perform, let alone even know about. How did Gayle get her hands on this?"

"That doesn't matter—what does the spell do?"

The light in Quinn's eyes dimmed until they lost all

luminescence, and she was back in the current world. She stared at Valeria with a mix of confusion and horror.

"This spell was used to drain power from other witches and transfer it to themselves. It was a method of extending life that was outlawed by the first ever coven of witches."

"But what does that have to do with Kenji?!" Valeria could feel her eyes spiking with tears. "That doesn't necessarily mean anything, and it's certainly not enough for him to be killed over it!"

Quinn shook her head as she handed the protective charm back to Valeria.

"I don't know, but it doesn't look good. You might be in more danger than you thought, Valeria. I would take every precaution you can."

"You should move in with me for a little while," Landon offered. "We'll swing by your house to pick up a few clothes and whatever else you might need, and you can hide out there until we figure out what to do next."

Valeria's head was reeling with this new revelation. She didn't only receive confirmation that Gayle was the one who tampered with Kenji's protective charm but also discovered that she had potentially altered his memories. Her entire world was flipped upside down; all she could do was hold onto Landon's arm and squeak out one tiny word.

"Okay."

ELEVEN

Suspicions Arise

RING... RING... RING...

Gayle frowned at her phone as she was sent to voice-mail again. The automatic message played softly from the speaker, informing her that the recipient was unavailable at the moment but would take a message at the tone. She cleared her throat as she left her third message in two days.

"Hey there, Valeria. I'm just calling again to check on you. I know things have been rough for you recently, but I would love to hear from you again. Maybe we could go out for lunch—I've been in and out of the hospital for the past couple of days, but I'm sure I'm past the worst of it."

She studied the back of her hand, frowning even more profoundly at the liver spots and signs of age. Of course, it's only natural for humans to grow older and for their bodies to decay. Nonetheless, she figured that the witch community would have come up with a remedy for that by now. It didn't really matter, though—what they did come up with would have to suffice for now.

"Anyway," she continued, "please call me when you can... I love you."

She disconnected the call and set her phone on the kitchen table. Her suspicions grew stronger each day that she didn't hear from Valeria. First, her granddaughter acted strangely at their lunch the previous week, and now she was avoiding her entirely. She couldn't help but mutter ominously to herself at the thought of...

"What's on your mind, Gayle?" a cool voice floated in from the other room. After a moment, Sadie emerged from the living room, where she got herself busy with some task —just like she had been doing for the past two weeks. Her sharp eyes peered at her grandmother curiously as she took in her worried demeanor.

"It's nothing, my dear," she answered with a level voice. "I think my hip is acting up again, that's all."

Sadie raised an eyebrow at her, clearly not buying the lie. Regardless, she shrugged and returned to whatever she was working on in the other room. Gayle understood that her granddaughter was taking on a very weighty burden by helping her out with all of this. However, she still wished she could get at least a small hint of what she was doing now.

Not wanting to let her restlessness get to her, Gayle got up from the kitchen table and ambled meekly over to her spell room. It was maddening to have such unfathomable power trapped in such a frail, broken body. She was among the most powerful witches in the United States, possibly even the entire world. But look at her now—reduced to a death-sentence sickness and aching joints.

Gayle opened the door to a dark, musty room tucked away at the side of her house. She hadn't been there since... Well, it would suffice to say that she hadn't been there in a while. The air in the room was stale, and there was a light covering of dust on everything. It coated the worn green couch, the coffee table with the broken leg, and the Grimoire that she still hadn't returned to its proper place on her bookshelf.

She sat down behind the table and picked up the book of magical spells and incantations, feeling the hefty weight of it in her weathered hands. This particular grimoire was an original spell book owned by the first-ever coven of witches. She could still feel the remnants of their boundless power even now, thousands of years later. It lay dormant in the pure leather binding and cloth pages, only seeping out when she opened it to reference a spell or look up an incantation.

The grimoire was already open, of course. As a matter of fact, it was open to the exact page that she was reading when that bastard of a man walked in on her unannounced—spouting some nonsense about an extended family cookout. God, if he had just exercised a modicum of restraint and used his manners, then she wouldn't even be in this mess to begin with!

But there was no sense in agonizing over any of that now. What had happened had happened, and even a witch as powerful as her couldn't change the past. So far, she had taken every precaution and change of plan in stride, and everything had still been going according to plan. Her granddaughter's potential suspicion of her might cause a little bit of a hiccup, but it was not something that she couldn't be able to deal with.

She set the book back on the table, subconsciously leaving it open to the page detailing the spell and ritual she needed to perform to steal another witch's power. In essence, the ritual would also transfer that person's life force, giving Gayle just a little bit more time to solve the predicament of imminent death.

The rest of the table was clear, but she wasn't concerned about the whereabouts of the other items for the ritual. She had locked the vial of blood and bundle of hair in a nearby cabinet. In contrast, another small vial containing tears of joy was kept in a refrigerated box hidden in a wall safe. She only needed one more ingredient —the ashes of a Gryphon—before her list was complete. Thankfully, she had a few contacts that knew where to find such a rare item, and it was on its way to her now in an express-shipped box.

That wasn't the most difficult part of the ritual, though. The hardest part was something that she struggled with for months on end after she discovered this confounded page in the grimoire. It required the greatest sacrifice known to witch-kind and possibly the greatest sacrifice to her personal relationship with Valeria. To complete the ritual, she needed to sacrifice the loved one of her loved ones.

There weren't many people in her life that fit such criteria. Valeria was the only one of her kin with a partner, and her granddaughter would undoubtedly be considered a 'loved one.' Unfortunately, that meant that Kenji was the only person who could be sacrificed, which Gayle initially refused to even entertain as a possibility.

She tried for the longest time to find some other way, a different spell, or maybe even a different method that could take the original's place. In the meantime, she prepared all the items for the ritual she needed in case she stumbled across something. Then Kenji walked in on her and started asking questions; everything happened so quickly after that.

Gayle had jumped up from her table and immediately cast a memory-wiping spell on him, instructing him to forget that he ever walked in on her in the first place. She thought it had worked, too, until Valeria casually explained that Kenji was acting strangely while they were having lunch. The memory must have been scratching its way to the surface since it directly involved the woman he loved most.

Kenji was trying to warn her. She had no choice. She had to act.

Getting Sadie to use her blood magic and make her granddaughter's husband walk into the river was one of the hardest things she ever had to do. But strangely enough, with the pain came a sense of relief. Her choice had been made for her, and she covered her tracks in this awful affair. Apparently, she hadn't covered them well enough, though.

"Hey Sadie," Gayle called out warily, "can you please come in?"

It only took a moment for Sadie to sail down the hall and into the spell room. She had the same indifferent look as before, but Gayle could tell that her granddaughter was worried about her. Sadie had always been good at hiding her emotions, but Gayle was even better at seeing through her stoic guise.

"It's okay," she motioned for her granddaughter to join her at the table. "You don't have to worry about me. I'm fine."

"Well, what is it then? I'm pretty busy with… Well, I'm just busy. Let's leave it at that."

Gayle couldn't help but sigh.

"It would make me feel a great deal better if I knew what you were doing in there."

"Trust me, you wouldn't feel better. Just leave all that stuff to me and let me take care of it. Now, you called me for something?"

Gayle subconsciously ran her hand over the open page in the book, noting that it was just as wrinkled and old as the fingers that touched it.

"I can't help but feel concerned about Valeria," she started, unsure where to go from there.

"I wouldn't worry too much. I know she just lost her husband, but she's an adult, and she knows how to take care of…"

"That's not what I mean, Sadie. I mean, I am concerned that she is onto us. She knows something. I can feel it in my bones."

Sadie pursed her lips as she thought deeply about this.

"What makes you think that?" she asked concisely.

"She hasn't returned my calls and was acting strangely at our lunch the other week. I felt like she was watching me like a hawk, analyzing my every word and movement, just waiting for me to slip up so she could drag me down."

"I think you're worried over nothing," Sadie answered casually. "Valeria has always been strange like that, and I'm sure she's only acting even stranger now out of grief."

Gayle rose from the table, and with her rose an extraordinary presence. It seemed to grow and grow until it filled out the room and made the old woman appear larger than life. Sadie was no longer in the presence of her grandmother but rather a powerful witch with incomprehensible magic that eclipsed all else. When the old woman spoke, it was with the authority of a god.

"I am not susceptible to aimless worries or elderly whims. There is something devious brewing—I can feel it just as surely as I can feel the spirit of my ancestors and the powers that dwell within me."

With that, the intimidating presence waned, and Gayle withered back into an aged and dying woman. Sadie managed to keep her composure the entire time, but she couldn't help but feel as if she just had a scrape with death herself. She drew in a deep breath and faced her grandmother head-on.

"Alright, I hear you. If you think Valeria is onto us, then I believe you."

Gayle smiled weakly at Sadie.

"You do?"

"Yes, I have a plan, but we must act fast."

TWELVE

Investigation

V ALERIA

"This seems like a little much, Vale."

Landon and Valeria were crouched around the corner of a house that she believed belonged to the owner of the fresh market. That's not why they were there—they were using the cover to peer at the house across the street and keep an eye out for any signs that Gayle or Sadie was home. Valeria was busy searching through the house with her powers when Landon spoke up.

"You're free to leave any time you want," she responded without accusation because that was the trust. Landon didn't have to accompany her for any of this; he could cut all ties with this mess instantly if that was what he wanted. She couldn't blame him for that, especially if he was scared about this.

"I'm not going to leave! It's just... I'm unsure how comfortable I feel facing off with a witch as powerful as Gayle."

"Well, you don't have to worry about that," Valeria pulled her powers back and stood up. "I checked the whole place twice now, and it looks clear. I'm not sure how much time we'll have until they return, so we must hurry."

The pair casually crossed the street and moved to the side door tucked away toward the back of the house. They didn't want to arouse any of the neighbors' suspicions. If anybody asked, she would just tell them that she was popping in to drop off something for her grandmother. Luckily, they managed to open the door and slip inside without coming across any assailants or peeping Toms.

The inside of the house was as still as Valeria's powers perceived it to be. Nobody was home.

Valeria and Landon immediately launched into action, not wanting to waste any time. Their plan was to search for the items Quinn saw in Kenji's memory: the vial of blood, sparkling clear liquid, and hair bundle. While she trusted that her husband stumbled across Quinn's profane ritual, she also understood that memory could be a finicky thing. Before moving forward with her plan, she would have to confirm the items for herself.

Landon headed off toward the back of the house while Valeria went straight to the spell room. He spent three hours the previous day trying to convince her to let him accompany her, but she knew they would have limited time to explore the house. He would have to be content with splitting up until they discovered what they wanted to do and put his trust in her to protect him if it came.

Valeria slowly pushed the door to the spell room open while wincing at how loudly it creaked on its hinges. She could hear Landon's footsteps in the other room cease for a moment as they both kept an ear out, but no assailant responded to the raucous sound. She moved quickly into the room and tried to push down her sense of reminiscent longing at the memories she and Gayle created there.

She figured that her grandmother would have hidden

the items for her ritual if she knew she was found out. That's just the person she always was—very careful in her planning and methodical in her clean-up. Valeria briefly recalled how Gayle would sing a specific song when the two of them would clean up the house every Sunday and shook her head.

That's not the Gayle she was dealing with right now or the grandmother she knew and loved. She had to focus.

This was the only room that she couldn't reach with her powers. She already knew that Gayle kept a protective seal over her spell room. Hence, she figured that seeing into it was a long shot anyway. Even now, as she was standing inside it, she couldn't stretch her powers outside her own body. She bit down on her lip in frustration and decided to do things the old-fashioned way: by searching with her eyes.

The first thing that drew her attention was the large cabinet to her left. Gayle kept all sorts of odds and ends in there to help with her rituals, but she kept most of the drawers locked. Valeria tried each of the handles individually, just as she figured. None of them budged.

She needed to find out where the keys to the drawers were. Gayle had undoubtedly used them in front of her before, especially when she was teaching her spells from her grimoire. Nonetheless, she just couldn't recall for the life of her what she did with them afterward. What she did know, however, was that she had a neat little trick up her sleeve that she had brought specifically for this venture.

She pulled a small folding device from her right pocket and a thin metal rod. The rod went into the lock on the far right, and while she held it there, she flipped through the different apertures of her device until she found the perfect size. It only took a few minutes of her tinkering around until she heard a click of the lock opening.

"Thank you, handy dandy lock pick," She sighed in relief.

She yanked the drawer open and pawed through it in a frenzy, but she could only uncover a stack of loose papers and a single brown rock. She moved on to the next drawer and then the next, slowly losing hope with each dead end she came across. Then she opened the last drawer in the cabinet and froze.

There was a bundle of hair wrapped in twine and a vial of blood on the top of a transparent box containing dried herbs. She lifted the two items carefully and peered at them closely. It looked like the blood had congealed, so it must have been old. As for the hair, there was a peculiar quality to it. The strands were dark brown, springy, and curly. Like a remnant of a fluffy cloud...

Dear God. It was her hair.

The shock almost made her drop the items, but she managed to hold fast to them. Her head was spinning as she broke out in a nervous sweat. So it was real. All of this was actually real. Gayle was preparing to perform this profane ritual, and Kenji discovered her plans. But she only had the hair and the blood. What about the...

"Valeria," Landon's voice came from behind her.

She turned and saw that he was holding out a small vial. A few drops of a clear liquid were sitting at the bottom, and when he tilted the vial, they sparkled in the light. It was precisely what Quinn had described in her vision.

"Where did you find it?" she breathed.

"I found it in a hidden wall safe." He folded the vial into his hand to hold it more securely. "I don't know why, but I figured she would have hidden these things secretly. My first thought was one of those old-timey wall safes—my dad has one, and the neighbor across the street from me has one. So it only made sense that she would have one too."

"But how did you manage to get it open?"

"I didn't have to. The dial was already set to the correct code." She caught a glimpse of sadness flash across his eyes before he continued. "My best guess is that Gayle put this in the safe and forgot to twist the dial after she closed it. She must really be getting old...."

"That doesn't matter right now," Valeria grabbed his arm and led him back to the side door. "We got what we came here for. Let's get out of here before either of them returns, and then we'll figure out what to do from there."

Sadie

"...so I think the next best bet would be to check the shop, and if that doesn't work, then we can ask the neighbors and go from there."

The voice came outside the front door while somebody fiddled with the lock. After a few moments, a click sounded as the door unlocked and swung inward. Sadie stepped forward, holding two large paper bags filled with groceries, while a weary-looking Gayle followed her inside.

"I don't think that she's gone into hiding because Gerard told me that he saw her the other day going out with..."

"Quiet."

Sadie turned and stared at her grandmother in surprise. While she was taken aback by the sudden admonition, she was caught even more off guard to see the look on her grandmother's face. Her eyes were wide with panic as her pupil's shrunk down to pinpricks, and her mouth was hung slightly open and quivering.

"Gayle? What is it? What's wrong?"

"Somebody was here!" she hissed in a tone riddled with fear and anger.

She watched as the old woman bounded into the house, suddenly filled with a vigor she hadn't seen in ages. Sadie calmly set the paper bags down on the ground. Inside she was panicking just as much as Gayle was. How could she tell that somebody was in her house? And how did she not sense them, even now as she was trying so desperately to?

"The seal on my spell room," Gayle answered as if she read her granddaughter's mind, "has been broken. Someone was in there... or might still be in there."

The two women froze as they stared at the door to the spell room down the hall. It was closed the same way that Gayle had left it before they went to pick up their groceries. Still, she trusted her grandmother's magical instincts to know when the seal she cast over it was broken. She strained her ears for the sounds of an intruder, but the only thing that broke the tense silence was the call of a nearby Blue Jay.

"I'll go first," Gayle murmured softly, but Sadie held a hand out to stop her.

"No, let me go. You've worked so hard for all of this. There's no sense in putting yourself in jeopardy now."

Gayle stared at her for a moment, obviously conflicted, but then she nodded in confirmation and allowed her granddaughter to lead the way. Sadie padded quietly down the hall, doing her best not to make a sound. She wasn't scared for her own safety—she had command over all blood magic and therefore command over the human body. Her main concern was her frail grandmother, powerful in spirit and magic but trapped in a body failing her.

So, she moved slowly, and when she got to the door, she looked back to ensure that Gayle was at a safe distance. She gripped the doorknob firmly, noting that she couldn't feel the usual flow of magic through it, and pushed the door inward. For a brief moment, nothing happened, and then she felt a force knock her sideways off her feet.

"Move," Gayle shouted as she sailed past her and into the room. Sadie hit the ground hard and was back on her feet in the next second. She wanted to ensure her grandmother wasn't in danger. She bolted inside the room to see Gayle fumbling with her cabinet keys in agitation.

"Gotta check…" she was mumbling, "gotta see."

She finally found the correct key and jammed it into one of the locks on the far-left drawer. In the same motion, she unlocked the drawer and yanked it open, wide eyes searching for the items she collected for her ritual. She could only see her box of dried herbs and a rock from the river.

She charged out of the room and down the hall with an animalistic scream. In just a moment, she found the spot where her wall safe was hidden, except it wasn't hidden anymore. The painting concealing it was on a nearby counter, and the safe door was hanging wide open to show an empty space where the tears of joy were. It took only a moment for her to realize what had happened.

She turned on her granddaughter with such a fury that the woman shrunk away from her in fear.

"Intercept the gryphon ashes, get my ingredients back, and capture that damned girl before she ruins anything else!"

THIRTEEN

Up in Flames

VALERIA JUMPED OVER THE FENCE, NOT EVEN WAITING FOR Landon to unlock the side gate. The second she landed on the soft grass on the other side, she felt a wave of peace and serenity wash over her. Landon's backyard was one of the most calming places to be. She was surrounded by a variety of nature. Apple trees followed the path of the birch fence surrounding the yard. Each square foot was dotted with a strawberry bush, a bundle of coral honey-suckle, or some other verdant foliage.

However, the calm only lasted for a moment before the reality of everything crashed on her again. She gripped the vials of blood and sparkling clear liquid in one hand while she gingerly handled the bundle of her own hair in the other. She didn't know why she took such care with the final item, maybe because it was an extension of her own body and deserved to be treated with care. But that wasn't right. These items were meant to carry out a profane ritual, so in that line of thinking, these items were unholy. Suddenly, it felt foul to even be in physical contact with them. Valeria set the items down on a nearby stone table and stepped back, pointedly turning her body away from them so she could face Landon.

"So…" she started, unsure about what to say. What could she say in a situation like this? Her grandmother, the woman who raised her from age ten and seemed to love her endlessly, had a part to play in Kenji's death. In fact, the more she thought about things, she was directly responsible for them.

"This is messed up," Landon answered as if he were reading her thoughts. "Like, seriously messed up. It's one thing to be suspicious of Gayle, but to find concrete proof that she had something to do with all of this? It just feels so wrong."

"I know."

For a brief moment, they stopped being adults. They regressed to feeble children wallowing together due to the betrayal of their shared mother figure. Even though Landon had a mother of his own, that didn't change the fact that Gayle treated him as if he were her flesh and blood. They were both hurt in the same way, and they needed some time to feel the raw truth of that pain.

Landon moved over and enveloped Valeria in a tight hug. She thought she could handle all of this, but the second his arms squeezed around her, she broke down. Her body shook with wracking sobs, and she clutched onto the front of Landon's shirt as if it were a lifeline. It felt as if her heart was breaking exactly as it did when she found out Kenji was gone.

"Why is this happening to me?" Valeria whimpered pathetically. "First, it was Kenji, and now this? It's not fair, Landon!"

He didn't respond, but she could feel his chest quiver as

he began crying. The two stood there holding each other and mourning their circumstances for a few minutes. They cried until they thought they couldn't cry anymore, and once their bodies exhausted the last of their tears, they pulled back and looked at each other.

"You have to act, Vale."

"Huh?" Valeria sniffled as she wiped the last of the tears from her eyes. "What do you mean I have to act? How?"

"You have to stop Gayle before she hurts anybody else."

Valeria recoiled in shock and took a step back.

"What?! No, Landon, how could you even suggest something like that?"

His bloodshot eyes hardened as he grabbed her by the shoulders and forced her to face him.

"She killed your husband. That's a horrible thing to say, but it's the truth. We have proof that she had something to do with Kenji's death and that she's planning on performing a life-stealing spell on another witch. Are you going to let her get away with that?"

Valeria started to tremble as she realized the gravity of what he was implying.

"I… I can't." She whispered in horror. "That's my grandmother you're talking about. Even if…no, even though she did all these horrible things, I still can't bring myself to hurt her. Moreover, she's already losing her strength as it is…"

"No, don't think like that. Don't view her as the frail, loving woman who raised you because that's not who she is anymore. She is the person who ended Kenji's life and will end somebody else's life if you don't do something about it."

"Why me?" She could feel the urge to cry again even though she had no more tears left. "Why do I have to be the one?"

Landon softened then and released her.

"It can only be you, Vale. You're the only one who knows what she's planning on doing. And even if you could get in contact with other witches, it might be too late. I suppose we could try to get Quinn to help…"

"No!" Valeria cried out. "We can't. She's worked too hard to hide from the rest of our kind. If I enlist her help in all of this, I risk exposing her."

Landon pressed his lips together and looked at her expectantly.

"So, if Quinn isn't available…"

She knew what he was saying. She could see it in the pity in his eyes as his shoulders slouched with resignation. He had already accepted the reality of their circumstances that she struggled to recognize. At that moment, however, dejected and broken, she saw the truth.

"I'm alone in all of this. You're right. It can only be me."

"Well, you're not technically alone," he said with a soft smile.

Valeria nodded appreciatively. That was also the truth —she technically wasn't alone when she thought about it. Landon was helping her to the fullest extent of his mundane abilities. Even though Quinn was limited in her services, she still lent them the assistance they needed without a second thought. That gave her the assurance she needed, and she nodded once again.

"You're right. Thank you, Landon. I feel a little bit better now."

"Good. Now that we have all the evidence we need, we

must strategize. Obviously, I'm willing to offer any and all resources I can give, but…"

"Wait." Valeria held a hand up to interrupt him. "I understand that I'm the only one who can act here, but I'm still uncomfortable with hurting my grandmother."

"Not just your…"

"I know she's not just my grandmother anymore; that's not what I'm referring to. Familial ties or not, Gayle is still an incredibly powerful witch. Even though her body fails, her magic is as strong as ever. I don't know how I could ever possibly face off against her."

"Well then, let's not think about that right now. Let's start with baby steps and do what we can for now."

He moved to the stone table and scooped the items in one hand.

"First, we can't let Gayle perform this ritual. If she doesn't have the necessary items, she doesn't have the means to steal her life from another witch. We have to destroy these."

He cocked his head as he looked at the items curiously, then lifted his arm above his head to smash the items into the ground. Valeria managed to whip her arm out in time and stop him on the downswing.

"Wait! Not like this."

He stared at her in confusion as she took the items gently from his hand.

"Ritualistic items can only be destroyed, and I mean properly destroyed, by magic. You can try your hardest to shatter these vials and grind the hair into dust on your own, but you won't get far."

Valeria moved to a bare spot of dirt toward the edge of Landon's backyard and set the three items down on it. She made sure to space them out so the two vials were side-by-side with the bundle of hair in between and just below them, forming a perfect triangle. To perform an annihilating ritual such as this, one had to utilize one of the most common shapes in nature and magic.

Landon stood by her side as she arranged the items, serving as an encouraging presence as she set about the ritual. She held her hands out, palms toward the triangle, and touched her pointer fingers and her thumbs together. With this, she made an upside-down V-shaped hole, peering intently at the items through the shape she created.

She called upon the force of fire from the deepest well of her magic. She could feel it burn its way up from the ground, sear through her feet and legs, and burn all the way out to her fingertips. Suddenly, the vials and hair burst into a brilliant flash of pure red flame, held only for a moment before it sputtered and flickered out of existence. What was leftover were three small piles of ash and the sour smell of burned hair.

Valeria felt a slight glow of relief in her chest now that the ritualistic items had been destroyed. She watched dark gray smoke rise from the piles of ashes and melded together, rising in one united plume toward the heavens. As she followed the line of smoke upwards, she suddenly saw an angry face glaring at her from the other side of the fence. Its eyes were wide with rage, and its mouth hung open as if it were screaming at her.

"What?" She peered through the smoke until the face came into focus, and she froze. "Sadie?"

It was Sadie, standing on the other side of the fence. She then realized that her strangely warped face wasn't staring at her but just off to her right. She turned to see Landon shaking violently in place, his face a deep red from straining. He was looking directly at her with desperation as he began to shake harder and harder. She didn't understand what was happening, but she could tell it wasn't good.

"Landon," she started, but it was too late.

In one swift motion, he brought his fist down on her and punched her as hard as humanly possible in the face.

FOURTEEN

Fighting Fire with Blood

VALERIA WAS SENT FLYING FROM THE FORCE OF THE HIT. She was so shocked that the pain of the punch didn't even register until she hit the ground. First, she felt the jolt of harsh stone on her hip, then the sting of gravel digging into her palms, and finally, a ring of agonizing pain lit up her eye socket.

She cried out in pain as she shot her hand up to cover her eye. As far as she could tell, the hit didn't damage her actual vision, but the pain was so immense it was almost dumbfounding. Her mouth began to water as an immediate wave of nausea washed over her. She stared at Landon in surprise as he continued to shake and grow redder in the face. He took a forced step toward her and let out a strained cry.

"Valeria," he gasped, "get... away from me. I'm not... doing this."

Those words were all it took for her to realize what was happening. She looked at Sadie's enraged face, then back to Landon, then to her cousin again. She was using her blood magic on him—her face wasn't enraged but rather intensely focused. And Landon was straining so hard because he was fighting her with every ounce of his being.

Valeria pressed the balls of her feet into the ground and rolled backward just as Landon clasped his hands together and brought them down on her once again. His fists struck the dirt right where her stomach was and left a deep imprint, indicating that Sadie was making him use his full mortal force. She was barely on her feet before he took another swing at her.

"Sadie!" she cried as she sidestepped his attack, "What the hell are you doing?!"

Her cousin didn't answer, and Valeria had to jump out of the way to avoid another one of Landon's attacks. Unfortunately, she wasn't as quick this time as she caught a forceful blow to the side. The breath whooshed out of her when she both felt and heard two distinct cracks coming from her ribcage. She staggered for a moment before falling to her knees.

She wanted to vomit. Of course, the pain was bordering on unbearable. Moreover, she wanted to vomit because this was all happening in the first place. She had no doubt that Gayle discovered the missing items for her ritual and sent her cousin after her. As to why Sadie would agree with this, she had no idea. It was apparent they had their emotional differences in the past, but to attack her outright like this was strange.

Valeria let her body fall to the side as Landon swung his leg up to kick her. She hit the ground on her good side and rolled just as his foot sailed by her face, mere inches from knocking her unconscious. She was back on her feet again and turned to face her friend directly.

If Sadie meant to attack her, she was going about it in the smartest way possible. Landon was objectively larger and stronger than her. There was no way that she could beat him under her control. And she knew better than anyone else how inescapably under her control he was. Even though Sadie could only control one person at a time, she had dominion over every single vein and blood vessel in that person's body. This meant that the only thing Landon had control over was his mind. He was trapped in his own body while that formidable witch used it against him, and the only thing he could do was try to fight against it with pure willpower. His eyes were tortured as he brought his fists down on her repeatedly.

She managed to dodge every single hit, but she knew she wouldn't be able to keep this up forever. Her injuries were draining her strength, and her stamina was starting to fail her. Every swift duck and sidestep made her heart pound faster and her breathing race. If she didn't stop this soon, he would overpower her.

"Vale," her friend spat out with great effort, "stop me."

"I'm not going to hurt you, Landon!" she cried out as he rushed her. She feigned to the left and managed to jump away to the right as he reached out to grab her.

"Don't hurt…" he uttered just low enough for her to hear, "just… stop."

Her mind went blank for a moment until she understood what he was trying to tell her. She was fighting him on the same level ground that he was fighting her on, but she didn't have to. She was a powerful witch with supernatural abilities! And while she vowed to never use her powers against anybody—especially her best friend—this seemed like a generally acceptable exception.

He turned on his heel and drove his elbow hard into her head. Again, the force knocked her to the ground, and for a moment, all she could see were stars. The same wave of nausea washed over her again, but she didn't have any time to succumb to it. Instead, she pressed her palm to the ground and unleashed her powers to the fullest of their extent.

She could feel every root and bit of foliage that surrounded her. Blood may have been Sadie's domain, but this was her playing field. When Landon took a step toward her, she sent a strong wave of her powers toward him, aimless in purpose, with the only intent of stopping him. A rush of branches that grew from a nearby sapling wrapped around his ankle, effectively holding him to the earth.

He dropped to his knees as his hands shot toward the branches, which is precisely what Valeria expected Sadie to make him do. With another surge of her powers, she made the branches grow onto his wrists. It only took a moment for her to bind his hands to his foot and bind him to the ground. He thrashed and flailed about, but even his massive physical strength couldn't compare to the power of her magic.

"Thank... thank you," he managed to get out before falling unconscious. His rigid body suddenly went limp and flopped to the side as Sadie relieved him of her powers, unable to use him further. Valeria wanted nothing more than to run over and check on her friend, but she still had an adversary to face off against. She rose to her feet and lifted her chin defiantly at her cousin.

"Where are the items for the ritual?" Sadie asked with a level voice. Even though she exerted immense power to control her friend, she didn't appear worn out or phased at all.

"They're not here anymore."

"Then, where are they?"

Valeria tilted her head and motioned to the three ash piles still smoldering in the dirt. It took a moment for Sadie to understand what had happened, but when she finally did, her eyes flashed with fury, and... it almost looked like fear. She turned her gaze back to Valeria and scowled at her.

"You brat! You have no idea how long it took me to collect those."

"So, you're in on this thing with Gayle, then."

"Of course I am," Sadie practically sneered at her. "She's dying, Valeria. Your grandmother is dying, and here you are trying to take away her opportunity to get her life back."

"By stealing the life of another one of our kind? By stealing the life of my husband?"

"He was a noble sacrifice in the grand scheme of something bigger than him. Besides, what's the value of a mundane life compared to that of a witch as great and powerful as Gayle?"

Valeria felt falter and stepped back from her cousin in disgust.

"Wha...how could you say that, Sadie? It doesn't matter whether Kenji was mundane or not. He was my husband! How could you let her take him away from me like that?"

"It's all for the greater good," her cousin shook her head as if she were explaining a basic concept to a petulant child. "You're just too blinded by your ineptitude to see that."

It hit her; just how far gone Sadie really was. At that moment, it didn't matter whether the woman in front of her was her cousin. She was blinded by whatever ideology Gayle sold to her. She was willing to do anything to give her what she wanted. This may have been her own blood that stood before her, but the blood of the covenant is thicker than the water of the womb.

"It doesn't matter anymore, Sadie. The ritualistic items are destroyed. You're not getting them back."

"Maybe not those particular items," her cousin responded as her eyes widened, "but I can always find others."

Valeria felt her body seize up as Sadie took control of her blood. She was so worn out from fighting Landon that she couldn't even use her little strength to fight it. Nonetheless, she attempted to break free from Sadie's magic. However, she could only manage to shake frustratingly in place just as her friend did.

"That's enough defiance from you now." Sadie casually brushed a strand of her hair back as she pointed to her car parked on the side of Landon's house. "It's time for you to come with me and stop causing so much trouble."

Valeria felt her body pull in the car's direction, and her right foot unwillingly took a forced step forward. She tried even harder to yank it back and run in the opposite direction, but she could only watch as her left foot followed, then her right again. She was helpless in the face of Sadie's overwhelming magic.

But then she thought back to her friend that she had left bound to the earth and remembered once again that she could level the playing field. While her magic certainly was strong, it was not as strong as her cousin's. Therefore, she had to go about this carefully if she was going to get out of this situation, but she only had a few moments to think.

Sadie opened the trunk of her car and commanded Valeria's body to get inside it. Her right leg folded into itself as she placed her knee on the back bumper, and as she leaned into the trunk, her cousin let slip a haughty laugh of Landony. Valeria wasted no time conjuring up a fast gust of wind, and she sent it forth with every ounce of her power while Sadie's guard was down.

The force was enough to knock her back a bit, but that was all she needed. Valeria felt Sadie's hold on her falter, and she used that small allowance of freedom to send gust after gust of wind after her. The first pushed her back a step; the second made her skitter backward, and the third sent her flying to the ground.

As she fell, Sadie's magic drew back entirely. Valeria immediately turned on her heel and sprinted toward a nearby tree line. It was about 50 feet away, and her cousin wouldn't be out of commission for long. She poured every last ounce of her strength into her legs as her muscles strained to get her to safety. Thirty feet now... twenty... ten...

With one final push, Valeria lifted free from the earth and landed amongst the trees. Her feet continued to pound the dirt as she whispered a quick incantation. Within only moments, she was cloaked to the sight and magic of any witch seeking her. She could hear a fading howl of fury and frustration as she took off deep into the woods, finally free from Sadie's assault.

"VALERIA?"

Landon stepped hesitantly around a nearby tree, doing his best to avoid the slick patch of moss at the base of it. When he finally came, he found that Sadie and Valeria were gone, and he regained control of his body. The branches that held him captive were gone, but in their place was this oddly steady breeze that seemed to push him toward his side gate.

He followed the wind's urging while figuring it was a

sign from Valeria. Once he exited his side gate, the breeze turned in the direction of the nearby tree line, and it continued to turn and guide him as he stepped deeper and deeper into the woods. It was only now that the gust of wind finally eased, and he was left somewhere a few miles away from civilization.

But of course, his instincts were right, and Valeria stepped into sight from around a bush when he called out to her. She looked awful—her hair stuck out all around her in a frenzied mess, and her right eye was starting to swell and darken with bruising. Guilt struck him deep in his chest as he went to apologize to her, but she held a hand out to stop him.

"There's no need to apologize. You didn't do this. Sadie did."

He watched as her eyes darkened, and a look he had never seen from her before came over her face like an ominous veil. She practically glowed with fury, and even his mundane senses could feel the rage and power emanating from her. Before him was a stronger, surer version of the Valeria that he had always known. And she was done being a pawn in her grandmother's messed-up scheme for extended life.

"You were right, Landon. The time for indecisiveness is over. Now, we fight."

FIFTEEN

Protection

A TALL FIGURE MOVED ALONG THE STREETS OF BARTON, wearing a long gray hoodie and a facemask that concealed his features from passers-by. If anybody were to look at him, they would assume that he had a cold and was out to pick up some medicine. He walked carefully as if he were worn out, but he was just being cautious.

At the same time, this man was walking through the streets while a smaller woman was ducking around alleyways and sneaking through people's backyards. Of course, nobody would see her doing so, as she was cloaked by a magical veil that hid her from both sight and supernatural senses. She was coming in the opposite direction as the man, but they were both headed to the same place.

Valeria knew that she couldn't let her grandmother or Sadie get away with attacking her. At the same time, she also knew that she could barely escape Sadie alone. She couldn't face off against the two of them without a plan. While she didn't have a plan just yet, she did know someone who might be able to offer some assistance.

A hanging bell chimed as the hooded man stepped through a shop door. Only two people were milling about, looking aimlessly at odds and ends that they were probably not going to buy. Behind the counter was a bored-looking old woman whose milky eyes lit up with interest when she caught sight of the man in the hoodie.

"Welcome to Fortune Favors," her aged voice dripped with curiosity. "What brings you here on this most mystical of days? A product? A service?"

"Possibly both. I would need your professional opinion on the matter, though."

The old woman's eyebrows raised slightly. After a moment, she threw a large smile and went onto the floor to talk to the other two guests in the shop. He could hear her making frivolous apologies and giving them half-baked excuses as to why she had to close up the shop early. Something about the stars was not properly aligned that day.

It took only a few moments for her to usher the two out, and once she locked the door behind them, she glided across the floor and led the man into the back room. He followed obligingly, ensuring not to disturb his surroundings as he stepped around while hanging ornaments and effigies. When he stepped into the room, the elderly woman was already replaced with Quinn's true form.

"What is it, Landon? Has something happened?"

"Yes."

The answer came from behind Quinn, and she practically jumped out of her skin as she whipped around to view the intruder. At first, there was nothing, but then Valeria seemed to materialize into reality from another hidden dimension. Quinn stared wonderingly at her for a second before frowning deeply.

"Jeez, Valeria, you nearly scared the life out of me! Give a chick a warning before you…."

She trailed off once she got a good look at her friend. Valeria's right eye was swollen almost entirely shut, and rimming it was one of the most severe bruises that Quinn had ever seen. Moreover, she was nearly covered head to toe in dirt, and she even had a loose leaf sticking out of her hair.

This was serious.

"Tell me what happened."

Quinn offered up one of her stools as she began pulling different odds and ends from a nearby drawer. Valeria took the offer gratefully and practically collapsed onto the seat, clearly worn out and on her last leg of strength.

"We were attacked."

"Yeah, that much is obvious." She set a perfectly spherical ball of garnet on the table and wrapped it in a fresh banana leaf. Once she pinned the leaf with a tiny sliver of bone, she gave it to Valeria, motioning for her to put it over her eye. The small woman did as she was instructed while she continued recounting what had happened.

"It was Sadie. She was sent by Gayle to retrieve the ritualistic items we stole."

Quinn nodded slowly, trying not to let on just how baffled and mortified she was by those two sentences.

"Um… okay. Maybe you should start from the beginning and then go from there."

"Right. After we left here the other day, Landon and I decided to investigate Gayle's house for ourselves. To see if we could find the items you saw for the ritual. We found them and took them back to his place so we could dispose of them properly."

"With conjured fire and the natural shape ritual, I presume."

Valeria nodded and shifted Quinn's offering in her hand.

"However, little did we know that Gayle was on our tail, and she sent Sadie after us. She used her blood magic on Landon to subdue me, and when that didn't work, she tried using it on me. I don't know why, but she didn't try to kill or hurt me. It actually seemed as if she were trying to kidnap me."

"Why would she want to do that when she could have easily just disposed of you?"

"I'm not sure. She said something about finding other items for the ritual, but other than my hair, I can't imagine what else she would need me for. Maybe to bring me before Gayle so she could do away with me herself. Maybe somewhere deep down, she genuinely couldn't bring herself to harm me. Who knows?"

"So, what's your plan from here?" Quinn motioned for Valeria to give the wrapped ball of garnet back to her, and when she removed it from her eye, she was glad to see that it was mostly healed. There were still signs of fading yellow from the bruise, but other than that, she would be fine.

"We're not exactly sure," Valeria responded evenly. "I know now that we need to take action, but I'm not exactly sure how to go about that. My first thought was to come to you to see if you might have anything to help us."

Quinn thought for a moment, closing her eyes as she searched the deepest recesses of her mind for an answer. Finally, she snapped her fingers and turned back to her drawer, pawing through it in search of whatever had come to mind. After a moment, she stood up and turned back to the pair, holding something out in each of her hands.

In her left hand was an oval-shaped stone smoothed out to perfection. Its base color was a creamy white, but that color was interrupted by multiple specks of rainbows that melted together and played tricks on the eye. Her right hand was basically the opposite of that—a jagged black rock flecked with violent red and orange. She handed the two to Valeria, who could feel their inherent power thrum through her the second they came in contact with her skin.

"What are they?" she breathed in wonder.

"Pure opal," Quinn pointed to the bright rock and then to the dark one, "and bloodstone. The former enhances powers if used with honorable intent, and the latter suppresses powers derived from dishonorable intent. In other words, you could enhance your own powers while subduing Gayle or Sadie's. Remember, however, that you can only subdue one witch's powers at a time, and the opal can prove fatal if used in offensive magic. You have to make sure you use them wisely."

"I'll," Valeria responded with the conviction of a war general.

Quinn couldn't help but widen her eyes in surprise. She had never seen Valeria like this before; it was as if something integral to her very being had been altered. The witch in front of her was powerful before, but this new confidence and conviction made her rise to the ranks of possibly even her grandmother herself. She nodded in silent approval.

"I wish I could do more for you, Valeria. I truly do. I would fight by your side to the bitter end if it didn't mean exposing myself to the entire world."

"I know you would." Valeria smiled comfortingly at her friend before rising from her seat. "This is perfect. I can't thank you enough."

With that, Valeria motioned to Landon, and without another word, the two stepped out of the room and left the shop. It was only then that Quinn allowed herself to bite down on her lower lip and sigh. Valeria could be as sure as she wanted, but even with the tools she had been given, she still had a hard fight ahead of her. She closed her eyes and prayed to whoever would listen that her friend would come out of this alive.

"So, what do you plan on doing with the stones?" Landon asked once they were a safe enough distance into the woods.

Valeria continued to walk silently for a few moments as she thought it over. She fingered the two stones in her pocket and heard the comforting sound of them clicking off each other. Quinn pretty much gave her the answer to her problems. She just needed to figure out the right way to go about it.

"We do what Quinn said," she eventually answered. "We'll figure out a way to meet up with both Gayle and Sadie in a neutral space. I'll use the bloodstone to suppress Sadie's magic, and while she's compromised, you will subdue her. Then I'll finally have the chance to confront Gayle about all of this and get some answers from her."

"It's still Gayle, though. She's immensely powerful—what will you do if she decides to attack you herself?"

At that, Valeria pulled the rainbow stone from her pocket and held it out for him to see.

"Then I'll use this to protect myself."

Landon pulled up short and held his arm out to stop Valeria. He turned and looked her gravely in the eyes.

"You heard what Quinn said, Vale. If it's used for offensive magic, it could prove to be fatal. Are you willing to risk the chance of killing Gayle if it comes down to it?"

Valeria fell silent once again as she thought through what he said. What would she do if it came down to that? Of course, she had the means to protect herself now, but was she willing to do so at the risk of her grandmother's life? She thought back to that howling voice in the river crying out for help, and the answer came to her immediately.

"Yes. I'll kill Gayle without hesitation if it comes down to it."

SIXTEEN

The Final Step

GAYLE SAT AT HER KITCHEN TABLE, DRAWING SLOW, DEEP breaths to calm herself down. She knew without a doubt that Valeria had broken into her house and stolen the ritualistic items. Maybe she even enlisted the help of that boy she'd been staying with as well. That was the only logical explanation for why all the items she painstakingly hid were found and stolen from her. Who else could it be?

That didn't matter, though. Even if Valeria did make off with the ritualistic items, she was still no match for Sadie. That was why she entrusted the blood witch with her plan to gain more power so that she could utilize Sadie's unending devotion to her.

She felt no shame in that. Her time was running out, and her resources could have been improved in this godforsaken town.

Gayle took her phone out of her pocket to check the time. She sent Sadie out on her task almost two hours ago, and the day was starting to grow dark. The thought that she might have come across some sort of snag or delay crossed the old woman's mind, but it was dispelled just as suddenly as it appeared. Sadie was sufficient enough to take care of herself. She was strong and calculative. She was a powerful user of blood magic, and she…

It is right outside.

Gayle's eyes sharpened as she focused on the door in front of her. She didn't hear her granddaughter approach the house, but she suddenly realized she could sense her magic on the other side of the solid wood door. It was as potent as the smell of freshly-baked lemon muffins or a chirping Blue Jay in the silent morning. Strangely enough, however, Sadie's magic was the only one she could sense on the other side of the door.

She waited impatiently for her granddaughter to enter the house, but Sadie stood outside. Now that Gayle was focused on her, she realized she could hear the woman shifting anxiously back and forth on her feet. That didn't bode well. Finally, Gayle scoffed in disgust and called out to her.

"I know you're there, Sadie, so how about you swallow your pride and face me like a witch."

The shifting sound stopped, and after a moment, Gayle watched the doorknob slowly turn to the left. Once it reached its limit, the door creaked open and revealed a guilty-looking Sadie. Her head was ducked down, so she couldn't meet her grandmother's gaze, and her face burned red with shame. As far as Gayle could see, Sadie was alone.

"Where is Valeria?"

Sadie audibly gulped as her eyebrows knitted together in agony.

"She's… she's not with me."

"Obviously, she isn't with you," Gayle responded through gritted teeth. "So if she isn't with you, then where is she?"

"I don't know."

"You don't know?"

"She managed to slip out of my grasp and take off into the forest. Before I could regain control of her, she donned a cloaking spell, so I couldn't follow her. At this point, she could be anywhere."

Gayle drew in slow and deep breaths again, trying to maintain her composure.

"I can find her. No cloaking spell is strong enough to deceive my magic. What about the ritualistic items? Did you manage to retrieve them?"

Sadie held a small, opened cardboard box out in front of her. Inside was yet another glass vial surrounded by soft pink packing peanuts. An almost insignificant amount of dark gray dust had settled at the bottom of the glass container, and Gayle's eyes widened as she recognized the rare material: gryphon ashes.

"Perfect," she whispered. "As long as we have the items for the ritual, we can still continue with our plan."

Sadie made an odd choking sound, and Gayle couldn't help but glare at her.

"What?!" she snapped venomously. "Spit out whatever damned thing you have to say and get it over with!"

"This is it."

Gayle froze. She remained a perfect ice sculpture of cold rage for a moment, but then she melted into a soft sardonic laugh.

"I'm sorry, my dear, I must have misheard you. It almost sounded as if you said this was it."

Sadie didn't respond. She simply continued to stare at the ground, with her eyes wide with terror.

"It almost sounded as if you told me that not only did you fail in capturing Valeria, but somehow you managed to lose the items I spent months painstakingly collecting without getting caught. But that can't be right, can it?"

"When I got there, she had already destroyed the items with ritualistic fire," her granddaughter murmured. "Then she managed to catch me off guard and..."

A loud bang echoed through the house as Gayle slammed her fist on the table. Then they heard another, then another. Sadie flinched as her grandmother continued to bring her manic fury down on the defenseless kitchen table repeatedly until she finally let out a terrible scream reminiscent of a banshee.

"I don't understand! How did you let her get away for destroying the items and then let her actually get away?"

"She had already destroyed the ritualistic items by the time I got there!" Sadie cried out desperately, imploring her grandmother to understand her side of the story. "And I almost had her, I promise! Right as I was guiding her into the trunk, she hit me with a gust of wind and..."

"Wind?!" her grandmother howled. "You mean to tell me that you suffered a mild breeze and lost your compo-sure?! You're a Gayle, for god's sake! You come from a long line of witches more powerful than your feeble mind can comprehend—how could you let this happen?!"

Sadie gathered a small ounce of courage then and lifted her chin.

"Because Valeria is a Gayle too. You may think of her as one of the weaker witches in our coven, but the truth is that her powers rival even mine. Yes, she is young but also learning fast and growing stronger. We just... wildly under-estimated her."

"Don't you ever presume that I am wrong, Sadie? If there is anybody that I have underestimated, it is you!"

Sadie couldn't help but flinch once more at such a harsh remark. She lowered her head again and cast her eyes to the ground, submitting to her position as an inferior witch. For a moment, the only sound in the room was Gayle's enraged, shallow breaths. Then the old woman crossed her arms defiantly and huffed.

"Well, like I said, I am never wrong. I don't believe that I underestimated you, and I don't believe that I underestimated Valeria, either. She simply got lucky this one time. We have more power combined in our sleep than she does in full consciousness. It's just a matter of going about this the right way."

"I promise that I tried my hardest to…"

"I'm not saying that you failed to go about your task the right way. Although, I'll admit that the thought of that little tree-hugging brat besting you would almost be laughable if the situation weren't so dire."

"She didn't… okay, fine. How do we go about this the right way, then?"

Gayle uncrossed her arms and opted to lean on her elbows instead. That was the question: what was the right way to go about this? They tried a full-frontal assault, but by the grace of whatever force gave witches their powers, Valeria managed to escape. If she was cunning enough to slip out of Sadie's grip once, then there was no doubt she could do it again, especially since she knew that they were coming after her now.

If an outright attack didn't work, maybe they needed to think more like Valeria and fall back on their smarts. She was currently cloaking her whereabouts with magic, which unfortunately made finding her more difficult. It certainly wasn't an impossible task for the likes of Gayle, but it would complicate things. So if they couldn't find her with magic…

"Alright," she finally responded with a sharp nod. "Let's try a different approach here. We would only waste time trying to seek Valeria out by supernatural means, so I say we confront her directly. We'll start by sending her a message requesting to meet."

"What?" Sadie's mouth subconsciously fell open. "I just attacked her after she discovered profane ritualistic items in your house—why on Earth would she trust either of us enough to meet up somewhere?"

"Because at the end of the day, she is still my grand-daughter, and I know her through and through. My guess is that she doesn't understand what's happening here, or if she does, she doesn't grasp the full extent of it. She's curious by nature, and she would want some answers. She will take the bait."

"But how exactly is it bait? Even if she does decide to meet with us, she'll still have her guard up. She already managed to escape once…"

"Thanks to…"

"Thanks to me, yes, I know. But as I was saying, she had already managed to escape once. That was when she wasn't expecting an attack. It'll be much more difficult to capture her now."

"I wouldn't concern myself with that. If you somehow manage to find a way to mess it up again, I'll be there to pick up your slack. She will not escape me. I can promise you that."

"She may not be able to escape you, but I can guar-antee you that she will put up a fight. I know you can handle yourself, but that doesn't mean I want to put you in harm's way… physically, that is."

"So we level the playing field. We'll ask her to meet us, where she will have limited access to natural resources. But it should be far enough from the town, so we don't draw unnecessary attention to ourselves. Maybe even a place where she has strong emotional ties that could also put her in a compromised mental state."

Sadie thought for a moment before she realized what her grandmother was saying.

"You're saying we should meet her at the river where Kenji died?"

"Of course. It's a plan that puts us at the highest advantage of success."

"I almost loathe to even bring this up, but wouldn't it be easier if we just... you know..."

Gayle stared at her granddaughter blankly for a moment before understanding her like a truck.

"We will not kill Valeria, do you understand? In case you forgot, she is a vital part of this ritual. I'll not risk my one chance at extended life due to your foolishness."

The anger that welled up in Gayle's chest didn't come from Sadie's suggestion but rather the idea as a whole. It enraged her that Valeria was interfering so much in her quest for a longer life. The fury that she felt toward her granddaughter was almost immeasurable. However, deep underneath all that, she realized she still loved her. This was why all of this was already hard enough without her meddling. Gayle would have to make a very difficult decision soon but would require Valeria to make that decision. So she closed her eyes and allowed her anger to build hotter and hotter until the blazing inferno disguised her one and only damning vulnerability—that pathetic morsel of maternal love that had done nothing but hold her back.

The time of weakness was over. Now she must act.

SEVENTEEN

Back to Where It All Began

THE TIME TO ACT IS NOW.

Valeria was unequivocally sure of it. When the realization came to her, it felt more like a universal truth than a passing thought. She couldn't help but sigh at the sheer inevitability of it all. Landon was sitting across from her, leaning anxiously forward on his knees, and the look he gave her was resigned understanding.

"It's time, isn't it?"

Valeria looked down at her phone and nodded—5:30 p.m., right on the dot. She swiped her finger on the screen and brought up the text message that Gayle had sent her a few days ago. Both she and Landon had read it numerous times since then, but it was so baffling that she couldn't help but go over it one more time.

Gayle: I want to meet with you at the spot where Kenji died. You have questions, and I have the answers—three days from now, at 6 p.m. precisely.

Valeria and Landon were tucked away in a hidden natural alcove that was a hundred feet from the river. They arrived there the day that Gayle sent that message, intending to wait beforehand just in case either Gayle or Sadie decided to set up a trap around the area. They took alternating shifts to allow the other one to sleep. Nonetheless, as far as they could tell, neither of the women tampered with the meeting area the entire time they were there.

As to why Gayle wanted to meet with Valeria, the answer was quite evident. Sadie had no reason to come after her of her own will, so it was very likely that Gayle wanted to meet to finish what they had started. She didn't feel like her grandmother would go as far as killing her, but then again, how would she know? Gayle killed Kenji, after all.

It's just... there was this feeling inside of her. This gut intuition told her there was something more to all of this that she couldn't see. Why Sadie would try to kidnap her instead of simply killing her was the first hint that something was off. Now Gayle wanted to meet up with her after she had sent her cousin to attack her?

Something definitely wasn't right about all of this.

"Do you remember the plan?" she murmured under her breath. She was standing on the tips of her toes so she could see down to the river bank, peering intently at the wide-open space.

"Yeah," Landon whispered back, "we're going to use the bloodstone to..."

"Shh!"

Valeria's eyes widened in terror as she cast her powers out around her once more, searching for another magical presence. Just like in the past three days, she didn't sense anybody, but that didn't mean they weren't out there. After all, Valeria was using a cloaking spell of her own—why wouldn't her adversaries be doing the same?

Landon pressed his lips together and nodded solemnly.

After a tense moment, Valeria relaxed, asserting they truly were alone. Even if her magical perception didn't pick up on a presence, the nature around them would have given one away. Skittering from a nearby squirrel, jolted branches from the sudden flight of a bird, or even the slightest crunch of fallen leaves were on her side.

She nodded once, and together they descended a slope that led down to the riverbank. After a few days of silence and observation, she felt as if their footsteps made far too much noise, especially considering how quiet it was that day. This part of the river was removed from the town, but even then, she figured she would hear the distant sound of conversation or doors opening and closing.

After a few moments, they stepped onto the riverbank. There they were, back to the place where it all began. Valeria couldn't help but squirm when she looked at where they had pulled her husband's body out of the river. She turned her head to the side only to find that Landon's bright eyes were peering agonizingly out over the water. He probably was reliving that same day from his own point of view. She gave his shoulder a comforting squeeze and turned around to face the rest of the riverbank.

Time was ticking down quickly. The two shifted anxiously on their feet, scanning the tree line for any sign of Gayle or Sadie. Everything was deathly quiet, save for the sudden sound of a fish flopping in the river. Landon jumped violently at her side, then grimaced sheepishly at her once he realized what it was.

There were only five more minutes left. After five agonizing minutes, Valeria would face the woman who tried to attack her and the woman who commanded her to do so. She felt more on edge than when she discovered the profane ritualistic items. Still, she just had so many questions for Gayle.

It was six o'clock. A heavy bell chimed somewhere off in the town direction, marking each hour's passing. After it clanged out six times, the clearing fell eerily quiet. A bird chirped in the distance, and the river babbled peacefully behind them. Every single muscle in Valeria's body was tense. After a short wait, she pulled out her phone and checked the time. It was 6:02 PM.

Her grandmother had never been late for anything in her life before. In fact, she was the one who taught Valeria the value of punctuality as both a woman and a witch and enforced it in every aspect of her life. Maybe this was a ruse to throw her off, or she got the location wrong. She rechecked the text to soothe her suspicions and shook her head.

"Where is she?"

Landon was just as tense as she was. He rolled his shoulders to calm himself down as he turned to look at her.

"I'm not sure. This is so strange. Maybe we should just cut our losses and leave."

"No!" Valeria hissed at him. "I'm not bailing out now. Not after everything we went through and how much planning we did. You can leave if you want, but I'm staying."

A muscle twitched in Landon's jaw as he clenched his teeth, but he shook his head at her nonetheless. He was indeed in this with her for the long run. Valeria turned back to face the clearing and reached out with her powers. She allowed the tendrils of energy to sneak over the earth, trying to keep a sense out for an approaching human form or possibly a source of magic.

Just like before, she didn't hear anything, and just like before, her surroundings didn't give away the presence of anybody either. Valeria huffed in frustration and crossed her arms. She didn't know what kind of mind games her grandmother was playing, but she didn't appreciate being toyed with.

"Maybe we should try calling her," Landon suggested, but Valeria shook her head. Things were already precarious enough. Instead, she sat down on the riverbed and crossed her legs, motioning for Landon to do the same. He took the spot to her right and sat down to wait alongside her.

And that's precisely what they did. They sat there and waited for almost an hour, feeling more and more that they would be stuck there forever. The sun lowered toward the horizon and had just made its bed amidst the trees when Valeria finally sensed something. There were two sets of soft and rhythmic thudding in the earth, just off to the left of them—footsteps, if she had to guess.

She rose to her feet before she could even think about doing so, and Landon was behind her in a matter of seconds. They watched as Gayle and Sadie emerged from the tree line and took a few steps into the clearing, eyeing their surroundings sharply. They didn't even look at Valeria until they were presumably satisfied that no traps had been set for them.

An odd feeling twisted in Valeria's stomach. There stood Sadie, her cousin, and the woman who had attacked her, and she didn't even look fazed to see her in the slightest. Her face was the perfect picture of poise and boredom as she shifted to put her hand on her hip. But that was always how she was—cold and controlled, even under volatile emotional circumstances.

Sadie was one thing, but seeing Gayle gave her a feeling that felt more like a punch in the gut. For one thing, her grandmother seemed just as frail and maternal as ever. She wore a light gray wool sweater and slacks, almost as if she were getting ready to turn in for the night instead of preparing for a battle. When she took a few steps forward, they were short and careful shuffles rather than confident strides.

It was also strange because Valeria was now looking at the woman she knew for certain had a part to play in Kenji's death. The kind old woman before her had tampered with her husband's memories so she could get away with what she did to him. To extend her life, she planned to perform this profoundly wicked ritual on some poor, defenseless witch.

"Gayle," she started to call out assertively, but her grandmother cut her off.

"None of that now, child. I'm sure you think you know what you're doing here, but I'll be the one to start this off."

Valeria wanted nothing more than to launch into the speech she had prepared, but she bit down on her lip and nodded. Gayle nodded back at her and glanced passingly over at Landon.

"It looks like I was right, then. That boy does have a part to play in all of this."

"Of course I do," Landon said in a strong and unwavering voice. "If Valeria is in danger, then I'll plunge into the deepest depths of my ability to protect her."

"I would be quiet if I were you unless you wish to die a violent and bloody death here and now."

Valeria couldn't help but flinch at the horrific words coming from her grandmother's mouth. She had never heard her say so much as an unkind word, yet, here she was, threatening her best friend's life.

"You will not speak to him like that." Valeria attempted to mimic Landon's fortitude as she lifted her chin up. "And you will not hurt him either."

"Oh, whatever, this whole thing is foolish anyway." Gayle lifted her hand and waved it as if she were swatting away a fly. "Do away with the boy, Sadie, and Don't let her slip away this time."

Beside her, Valeria could feel Landon tense as Sadie took a menacing step toward them. Just like in the backyard, the woman opened her mouth wide as if she were screaming, and her countenance took on an angry and manic expression. A few unchanging moments passed, and then Sadie's face slipped into a look of confusion.

Their plan had worked.

"Wha—" the woman started, but Landon was already charging toward her. In three bounding leaps, he crossed the clearing and jumped toward the astounded blood witch. Everything happened so fast that neither of the assailants could react. In one swift movement, Landon put his fist down and punched Sadie.

The impact was so sharp that a loud thwack reverberated throughout the riverbank. Sadie stumbled off to the left once, twice, then crumpled to the ground like a deflating bag. Gayle looked back and forth between Landon and Sadie in shock, then turned her gaze on Valeria. Her granddaughter was holding a deep red stone in her hand, and the look on her face was the most furious she had ever seen on her.

"Gayle Henry, I am here to bring you to justice for the murder of my husband and for plotting to steal the life of another witch. I know what I'm doing here, and you will answer my questions."

EIGHTEEN

All Powerful

GAYLE FLOUNDERED FOR A SECOND, STRUGGLING TO REGAIN control of the situation. She looked back to her grand-daughter lying still on the ground and felt a surge of anger pierce her heart. Why she ever thought Sadie could help was beyond her. The woman was weak, both in magic and physicality. Even though they were family, Gayle couldn't help but detest her at that moment.

"You ruin everything," she muttered darkly before turning back to her other granddaughter. "And you! How dare you come here and demand answers from me. I am the head of our coven and your elder, and I command respect."

"I don't respect murderers," Valeria answered coldly.

Another bolt of anger struck Gayle even harder than before. In fact, it was anger and something else. It had been a while since another witch challenged her, let alone her granddaughter. She had conflicting thoughts about how to view the woman in front of her. On the one hand, there was the little girl that she had painstakingly raised ever since she lost her parents. Conversely, the defiant witch seemed hell-bent on bringing her to justice.

'Justice!' She would just have to see about that.

"It seems you've forgotten who you're talking to, child. Not only am I the head of this coven and your elder, but I am also one of the most powerful witches alive. Let me remind you of this as I take what little you have left in this life."

Gayle turned her gaze on Landon then and focused all her attention on the bright ball of energy at her core. This is where she drew all of her power and why she was so powerful in the first place. It was like a metaphorical, volatile sun bursting at the seams with raw energy. Her pupils suddenly shrunk down to pinpricks, and she directed a violent burst of magic at the man standing next to Valeria. She smirked at this first Landony of many over her granddaughter, except nothing happened.

The two continued to stand there and stare down at Gayle with the confidence of an entire army. The old woman faltered before directing another bolt of magic at Landon, making it about ten times stronger than the first. Once again, nothing happened. She stumbled back in confusion and pointed a shaking finger at her granddaughter.

"What is this? How are you doing this to me?"

Valeria held her hand and showed off the dark red stone that Gayle had caught sight of earlier. It took a few moments for her to realize what it was, and when it finally hit her, she gasped. It was a bloodstone! She only ever knew one witch in her entire life with such a gem in her possession, and she went missing many years ago. How did her granddaughter get such a thing? Gayle thought.

"I'm sure you know what this is," Valeria called out, reading Gayle like a book, "and I'm sure you know what it does. You'll answer every question I have now, and I want you to honestly answer me."

Gayle breathed out in dismay as an entirely new feeling of uncertainty washed over her. For the first time in her life, she felt truly powerless. Not just because she was rendered powerless by the bloodstone but because she had no other means of protecting herself. Sadie was indisposed, and her failing body was by no means strong enough to fend off an attack. Suddenly, her surefire plan to capture Valeria had been turned on its head. And despite her rage and fear, she somehow felt a small spark of pride in her granddaughter for doing so.

"Fine," she asserted. "You got me. Ask whatever you want of me, and I'll answer to the best of my ability."

"Why did you send Sadie to kill me?"

Gayle was taken aback as a wave of confusion washed over her.

"What? I didn't send her to kill you. I sent her to kidnap you."

"Because I stole the items for that horrific ritual you're planning on doing? The one where you take the life of some innocent witch just to extend your own?"

Gayle realized then just how little Valeria actually knew about her plan. She knew that her granddaughter didn't have all the pieces! The old woman sighed and shifted her weight to her right leg, already feeling the exhaustion of her condition welling up.

"I didn't want her to kidnap you to punish you for what you did. I wanted her to kidnap you for the ritual."

Her granddaughter's face went blank then as she struggled to comprehend what she meant by that.

"What? Why do you think I would ever help you with something like that, Gayle?"

"It is because I Don't require your assistance with the ritual, my child."

Valeria's face remained blank, and Gayle could tell she wouldn't understand the implications of what she was saying unless she understood everything else.

"I suppose I should start from the beginning. As you know well enough, my body is failing me. The disease is sapping my energy and is practically draining my life like a bucket with a hole in it. There's nothing that modern science or medicine can do to save me, I'm afraid."

"You were never one to believe in such things anyways," Valeria responded carefully, still unsure of where her grandmother was going with this.

"You're certainly right. If anything was going to save me, it would be magic. And I searched everywhere, Valeria, you have to believe me. I tried all of the potions and incantations and traveled as far as my invalid form could handle... but there was nothing out there for me."

"Nothing except for this ritual, I presume."

Gayle nodded before pressing on.

"You may know about the ritual, but it doesn't sound like you know the full extent of it. To perform such a ritual, you need four physical items: hair, blood, tears of joy, and the ashes of a gryphon." Gayle scowled then at the motionless form on the ground next to her. "You have no idea how long it took me to retrieve that last ingredient, by the way."

"I don't care. You said the ritual required four physical items—what else did it require?"

Ah, yes. This was the difficult part.

"It requires the sacrifice of a loved one's loved one. In other words, I needed to take the life of a child, spouse, or friend of someone I care deeply about. Not many people in my life fit such criteria, Valeria. That's why Kenji had to go."

She watched as her granddaughter faltered and took a step back, reeling from what she said.

"But... Why, Gayle? I mean, I understand why, but how? How could you do this to me?"

"You never would have let me use him if you knew what I needed him for!" She cried out indignantly. "If it were between my life and his, I know you would have chosen him in a heartbeat. You would have fought me, just as you're doing now!"

Gayle started pacing as her heart rate kicked up, rising steadily with her anger as she recalled everything that had happened.

"Besides, I had to kill him after he stumbled on my preparations for the ritual. Even though he didn't fully understand what was happening, I could tell he knew it was bad, and he would have told you. If he had just minded his business, he could have gone peacefully! Instead, I had to have Sadie use her blood magic on him and make him walk into the river, all so it could look like a suicide and get you off our tracks."

She stopped and turned back to see that Valeria struggled to maintain her composure. Well, she had gone this far. She could take the final step, especially if it meant gaining an emotional advantage over her granddaughter.

"You asked me what else the ritual required—Kenji's death, sure, but there's one more thing. I needed a viable witch to steal life from, but the ritual had conditions. The life force must come from a witch with the rarest form of magic, a type found in less than 1% of our kind. For this ritual, I needed an elemental witch."

For a moment, everything froze. She watched as the man next to Valeria stiffened in horror while her granddaughter stood there. For that moment, no breeze sailed through the clearing; no birds chirped in the distance. There were just the three of them and that horrible revelation. Finally, Valeria broke the silence.

"You were going to kill me?"

The question came out as a pathetic whisper, and Gayle couldn't help but throw her hands up in exasperation.

"Of course, I was going to kill you, Valeria! Think about this from my perspective—you are the only witch who meets every criterion for the ritual. I collected the blood, hair, and tears of joy from you alone, and you have command over elemental magic. And if that wasn't enough, you had Kenji—the loved one of my loved ones."

"No," Valeria said a little bit louder in a trembling voice, "I'm not your loved one. I just can't be. If you truly loved me, you wouldn't have taken my husband from me. If you had ever loved me, you wouldn't have sent my cousin to attack me. But most importantly, if you loved me, then you wouldn't have ever even considered the possibility of killing me!"

Gayle rolled her eyes at her granddaughter and scoffed.

"Oh, please, I would have been serving the world. You have this deep well of power in you—an incredibly rare power, might I add—and what do you do with it? You run a dinky shop selling perfumes when you could be accomplishing greatness! You're weak and refuse to stand up for yourself, even now, as you're faced with your end."

"Hey, what the hell do you mean by that?!" Valeria's friend piped up as he took a step forward.

"I mean that I intend to go through with this ritual. I still have the gryphon ashes and can find a way to obtain the other ingredients. You will give your life for me, Valeria, and you will give it here and now."

Landon was about to speak up again when Valeria pushed him gently aside with her arm. She had this empty look in her eyes that didn't betray any emotion or thought that must have been running through her. She slowly lifted her gaze to meet her grandmother's and spoke.

"You're wrong, Gayle. I'll not give my life to you. I'll protect myself by any means necessary."

She lifted her other hand and held out a different stone. This one was white and sent out shatters of rainbows as the light hit it at many angles. Valeria drew in a deep breath; with it, she drew in essence from all four elements around her. She could feel the sturdiness of the packed dirt underneath her, the cool refreshing temperature of the river water, the lightness of the air, and the fire from deep within the Earth's mantle. She was filled with the power of the entire planet. Then, with a sharp exhale, she released all that power directly at Gayle.

A flash of white light was almost as bright as a lightning strike. It sailed out from Valeria's hand and struck her grandmother directly in the chest. The old woman flew back with the beam's force and landed about 15 feet away. Valeria dropped her hand and staggered from the sudden onslaught of exhaustion, and Landon was right there at her side to catch her.

"Woah, hey! Are you okay?"

Valeria used her momentum to shove herself away from him and stagger toward her grandmother. She was worn out and oddly sore, but she continued to push herself forward, step by step. Such mind-bending power surged through her, and to think that the opal only amplified it. Nobody could have survived such a blast. Nonetheless, she had to check.

When she reached her grandmother, the exhaustion became too much, and she fell to her knees. The first thing that caught her off guard was that the old woman's body was still intact. She hit her with so much power that she was certain she had ripped a hole through her. The second thing that caught her off guard was that her grandmother was still breathing. Gayle didn't die.

For some reason, that realization brought a sigh of relief. Apparently, after all of that—after the lies and the awful things that Gayle did and planned to do—she still loved her. Even though she still loved her grandmother, she couldn't forgive her. Landon walked up to her and wrapped an arm around her waist, bringing her up with him and holding her like a child.

"Come on, there's nothing left for us here. Let's go home."

NINETEEN

Forgiveness

VALERIA OPENED HER EYES SLOWLY AND DREW IN A DEEP breath. She felt extremely comfortable in Landon's guest bedroom that she didn't want to get up and leave. So she continued to lay there while looking around the room. She was smiling at all the little knick-knacks he had lying around and the fun pictures on the wall. The room almost seemed as if it were designed by a kid in an adult's body, which, now that she thought about it, actually described Landon perfectly.

"Rise and shine, Sleeping Beauty!" Landon said.

Speaking of the devil, Landon opened the door and peeked his head into the room. He had a toothbrush in one hand, and his hair was tousled from sleep. Valeria made a low groaning sound and sunk even further into the sheets.

"Nope, I'm not Sleeping Beauty. I'm Sleeping Gremlin." She wiggled until the blanket was wrapped entirely around her and stuck her head through an opening. "See? Just like a gremlin."

"Yeah, you do look like a gremlin."

"Hey!"

The two of them chuckled at the lame joke as Landon stepped fully into the room. He was dressed in a nice button-down shirt and slacks, and the sight of him reminded Valeria of her task for the day. He must have noticed that her smile slipped slightly because he grimaced and shrugged helplessly at her.

"Look, we obviously don't have to do what we're going to do today. You're an adult, and you know what's best for yourself. I just think that it would give you at least some closure before you…"

"I know," Valeria cut him off. She pulled the blanket down just over her legs and sat up. Her body was still incredibly sore from the events that happened three days earlier, and she still hadn't fully regained her energy. It almost felt like she was recovering from something as mundane as the flu. But what she had planned for the day reminded her that it wasn't anything.

"You're powerful, Valeria." Landon smiled broadly at her, and she could tell he was just as exhausted as she was. "I know I don't say that too often, but you are. I don't think I know anybody else who could have gone through what you did and come out intact on the other side."

"You don't know anybody else," she joked back, trying to keep the conversation light. "I'm pretty much your only friend around here."

"Yeah, Barton is a dead town. I almost envy you for leaving."

With that, he slipped out the door and left, presumably so he could wait for her to get ready and join him. Valeria sighed and slipped out of bed. She pulled on a light blue sweater and a pair of jeans, aiming to be as comfortable as possible for something that would make her wildly uncomfortable.

She didn't waste any time getting Landon, and soon enough, the two of them left the house and took off down the street. They made sure to take slow and even steps, and Valeria counted them to keep her mind off of what they were about to do. There was bleakness around them as they stepped up to the hospital entrance.

All nurses knew Valeria's face by now, and when she stepped through the doors, the closest one motioned down the hallway behind her, indicating where she should go. She took Landon's arm as they made their way down the corridor, peering into each room until they found the one they wanted. With a deep breath, she crossed the threshold and grimaced.

"Hey, Gayle."

The old woman didn't respond. She couldn't, as she had been trapped in a coma since their fight. Her body looked withered and frail when the strong soul wasn't present. Liver spots marred her bony hands as the machine attached to her mouthpiece pushed air throughout her lungs. She couldn't help but notice the obvious presence of ribs pressing up against her hospital gown.

It was a strange sight. Not just because Gayle had tried to kill her the other day but because Valeria couldn't think of a time when her grandmother looked weak. Even when her body started failing, Gayle possessed a commanding presence that rivaled that of gods and goddesses. Yet here she laid, indisposed and invalid.

Valeria didn't even know how she was supposed to go about this. She wrung her hands together and then shoved them in her pockets. When that didn't suffice, she pulled her hands out again and started picking her nails. Landon nudged her gently, encouraging her to begin. She craned behind her, making sure nobody heard, and sighed.

"Uh, okay," she started awkwardly. "Gayle, I am here

not because I wanted to see you but because I need to tell you something."

She watched as her grandmother's chest rose and fell robotically, then looked at Landon in despair. He nodded patiently and offered a faint smile. In a sense, he was telling her, 'There's no getting around this. You just have to go through it.' She drew in another deep breath and pressed on.

"What you did to my husband, what you planned on doing to me, is appalling. Even after witnessing it firsthand, I still can't believe you could possess such evil in your heart."

A different machine emitted three quick beeps as it updated the information about her grandmother's vitals. Her heart rate remained exactly the same, as did her breathing.

"Despite all of that, I want you to know that I forgive you. At the end of the day, you weren't my grandmother betraying me, but rather a scared and hopeless woman at the end of her rope. You did what you did out of fear, out of necessity. And because of that, I may believe again someday that you really did love me."

Her eyes began to spike with unshed tears, and she let out a small shaky breath.

"But forgiveness doesn't change what you did to me, Gayle. Even after discovering what happened to Kenji and bringing you to justice, I am still in such unfathomable pain. I feel like I'll live in it forever—unable to escape it, unable to grow or heal."

"So I'm leaving. I'm heading to the airport in the next town over tomorrow morning, and I'm leaving Barton. I don't know where I'm going, but I know that I can't stay here anymore. I can't continue to live in the same place where my husband was murdered and my own blood betrayed me. So I came here to say my final goodbyes. I'll not come back after this, and even if you wake up someday, you will never see me again."

Before she could process her emotions or give herself the chance to change her mind, she turned on her heel and strode out of the room. Landon was right on her heels, and they exited the hospital for the last time. The second Valeria was outside, she let out a pent-up breath and keeled over, putting her hands on her knees.

She wanted to vomit. She wanted to laugh. She wanted to cry, to scream at the top of her lungs, to take off at a sprint and not stop until her body physically gave out underneath her. A simultaneous wave of relief and pain scoured her entire body as she was finally washed clean of Gayle Henry, the woman who made her stronger and broke her down simultaneously.

No matter what, she would start her life again on a clean slate. She couldn't have moved on without letting Gayle know her true feelings, even if the old woman was barely clinging to life and unable to register her words. She wouldn't even have been able to do so without Landon by her side. He was the one who persuaded her to do this in the first place, and he remained a solid rock for her the entire time. She straightened up and looked him in the eyes.

"Thank you, Landon. Thank you for everything," Valeria said appreciatively.

He beamed at her and nodded.

"Of course. You're my best friend, and I'll always be there for you, even through whatever comes after this. We should probably get back home so you can finish packing. You have a big day or a great life ahead of you!"

Landon chuckled, but Valeria lifted her eyes to the sky and didn't respond. She could feel a tension in the atmosphere, the strain of something not settled yet. Of course, she resolved her grievances by speaking with her grandmother. However, there was still one more business to attend to before she could finally move on with her life.

"Come with me, Landon. I have to take care of something before we head back home."

She led him back down the street they came on, but instead of continuing toward Landon's house, they turned left and headed further into town. After about 10 minutes of walking, they entered Quinn's Fortune Favors shop. The windows were closed by drawn curtains, and as far as they could tell, the shop was closed to visitors.

Instead of heading through the front door, Valeria led Landon to the side of the building and around to the back. There, they came upon a beautiful garden with fresh fruits and flowers. In the center of it all was Quinn in her proper form, and when she heard the approaching steps of her visitors, she turned and flashed them a bright smile.

"Landon, it's nice to see you again. Valeria, I've prepared everything that you asked me to."

Landon stared down at Valeria in confusion, but she simply stepped forward and reached out to her friend. Quinn reached her own hand out in return and dropped a few small items into Valeria's upturned palm. When she drew her hand back, Landon could see that Valeria now held three smooth gray stones. It took him only a moment to realize what they were: river rocks.

The two witches sat in the grass, facing each other, and in one simultaneous movement, they crossed their legs and put their hands on their knees facing up. In Valeria's left hand were the river rocks, and in Quinn's right hand was the same opal she had given the two just three days prior. Together, they murmured an incantation under their breaths until a cloud above them parted and allowed a ray of sunlight to beam down on them.

Landon cocked his head to the side, his eyebrows creasing together in confusion. It was strange, but when the cloud parted and the two women lit up in sunlight, he could have sworn he heard a voice. Its timber was deep and masculine, yet soft as if it were a passing whisper in the wind. He could have sworn that it came from Valeria's direction, but he could only catch two words before it faded.

Thank you.

At that moment, he saw his friend's tension melt out. All of the pain and heartache she went through just seemed to seep out of her until all she was left with was a contented smile. She opened her eyes, and for the first time in weeks, he saw a glimpse of genuine happiness in her eyes.

"Alright, Landon, that was all I needed. We can go home now."

TWENTY

The End of It All

VALERIA SHIFTED BACK AND FORTH UNCOMFORTABLY ON her feet. She always needed to remember how busy it was in the city. The airport was filled with hundreds of voices that cascaded over one another. She couldn't look anywhere without coming across someone bustling around or sitting down, scrolling through their phone while they waited for their flight. Landon noticed her discomfort and nudged her gently with his shoulder.

"Hey, I know it's a lot, but remember that this is a good thing—your fresh start, your new adventure. Do you have your toothbrush?"

"Yes."

"Deodorant?"

"Yeah."

"Toothpaste? If you forgot, I could easily run back to my house and…"

"Jeez, Landon, would you relax? Your unhealthy obsession with my hygiene isn't making this any easier."

"Hey, I'm not obsessed! I just know that you'll be

hopping from hotel to hotel while you figure out where to stay, and they Don't provide that kind of stuff for you."

"I've been in a hotel before; they have those little complimentary bottles of shampoo and conditioner and stuff in the bathroom. I'm sure they'll have a little deodorant and toothpaste."

"Yeah, but not a toothbrush. If you forget yours, you'll have to buy it from them for like 25 dollars. Who charges 25 bucks for a skimpy little toothbrush, anyways? It's just ridiculous!"

The two fell silent after that as they watched the crowd move around them. She knew that his concern wasn't really about her hygiene products. All she had was a back-pack full of clothes and a few belongings she was taking with her, and Landon checked that three times before they left the house. Everything else that wasn't necessary, she was leaving it behind.

"Did you manage to get your house sold in time?" Landon asked again.

"Yeah, the guy that lives next to the butcher shop said that his family is expanding, and his little cottage can't keep up. I sold it to his son, who paid for the whole thing upfront and with cash, which I'm not even going to bother looking into."

Landon laughed at that and put his hands into his pockets.

"I can't imagine he could be up to any shady business, especially in a town as small as Barton. Even if he was, you know that all the old crones who attend church every Sunday would get together and spread the rumor like wildfire."

"Yeah, you're right."

Another beat of silence again, but Landon apparently wasn't finished.

"What about the shop? I know you struggled to figure out what to do with it."

"Oh, Quinn actually helped me out with that one. As it turns out, she wants to separate her work and her magic, which is ironic considering her work is magic, but whatever. She's taking over and converting the shop into a sort of holding place for her more important magical items."

"Hey, that's great! Now not only is your beloved shop taken care of, but it's also being left in the hands of someone you know and trust."

"Yeah," Valeria shifted again and moved her backpack to her other shoulder. "She offered to stay in contact with me to keep me updated on the condition of the building, so that's nice."

"That's nice. She's a good friend."

She side-eyed her friend and nudged him the same way he had nudged her before.

"She also offered to keep an eye on you, which is what I know you're actually worried about."

Landon bit his lip and didn't respond right away.

"We never got to find out what happened to Sadie," he finally mumbled.

And he was right. They left Gayle and Sadie in the clearing that day, intending to return the next morning to retrieve their bodies. However, when they got there, Gayle was the only person there. Sadie must have woken up at some point and seen her grandmother's condition, thus, causing her to flee the scene before she could meet the same fate.

They had searched everywhere for her. Valeria and Landon went to Gayle's house, but the place looked untouched since the two women were there last. The only notable difference was that Sadie's room was in shambles. A decent amount of her clothes were missing, indicating that she hurriedly packed her things to go into hiding.

They had also spoken to the townspeople, who didn't catch wind of the witches' fight at the riverbank. None of them saw what had happened to Sadie or where she went. Nonetheless, they all expressed their condolences to Valeria for her grandmother's condition. Like Landon mentioned earlier, word spreads fast. Therefore, she assured them that she and her grandmother were fine before leaving them forever.

"Quinn is a strong witch," Valeria assured her friend. "Like I said, she's stronger than me and almost as strong as... well, you know. She likes you, too, so even if she wasn't doing it for me, I could promise she would keep a close eye on you."

"Wha...she likes me?" Landon's entire face went red as he stammered over his words. "How do you know that; did she say something or..."

Suddenly the intercom overhead crackled as a female voice issued an announcement.

"Flight 131 to Nile, Washington, is now boarding. Please form two lines in descending order of seating priority and have a nice flight."

The intercom clicked as the message ended, and Landon heaved a great sigh.

"Nile, huh? Of course, I understand the similarities in names, but why else did you decide to go there?"

"Quinn told me that a woman in her coven lives there. She specializes in magic with ties to emotion, and I think she can help me healthily process my grief and move past it. I can't start my new life before I heal from my old one, and besides..." she smiled sheepishly at Landon before continuing. "It'll be nice to have a place to stay for a little bit—that isn't a hotel that overcharges you for toothbrushes."

Landon smiled down at her and pulled her into a tight hug.

"I'm going to miss you, Valeria."

"I'm going to miss you too, Landon. You're free to visit me any time, as is Quinn. Maybe the two of you could plan something together and make a road trip out of it or something."

She pinched her friend jokingly in the side before letting go of him. He stood there the entire time she waited in line, waving at her every few minutes and flashing a huge encouraging smile. Finally, she got to the front of the line and got her ticket checked. She waved one last time at Landon and stepped onto the boarding bridge.

Valeria took her seat toward the back of the plane and let out a breath. She had this strange feeling sitting at the bottom of her chest all day. Here she was, about to leave everything that she knew behind—the town where she was raised by the woman who betrayed her, the place where her husband started a life with her and died and where her friends encouraged her and stood by her side throughout this challenging moment of her life.

She recalled the very first day she met Kenji. He had come into her shop, and from the first moment she laid her eyes on him, she just couldn't bring herself to look away. He was so charming from the start, taking every opportunity to make idle chit-chat with her while he perused the different merchandise. He told her that he was shopping for a girlfriend and asked for her preferences, and when he checked out, he handed the small bottle of perfume to her with a wink and said, 'Here you go, sweetheart.' That was how it all happened; it almost took her by surprise. She didn't expect this, at least not in the way Kenji had adopted. Nonetheless, it happened, and she was glad to have him in her life.

She recalled the faint pain of losing her parents and her subsequent peace and love when Gayle took her in. When she closed her eyes, she could see all the times that her grandmother made her a delicious lunch or taught her a new spell. She could see the kindness in her eyes, even now, and she wondered once again if her grandmother ever truly loved her.

She thought about her shop, her friends, and all the lovely flowers and foliage in Barton, Florida. And once she was done thinking about everything that happened in her life, she tucked away all the places she went and the things she experienced in a little box at the back of her brain. She envisioned locking the box with a key and throwing it into oblivion, never to be seen again. Then, with a soft sigh, she opened her eyes.

The plane rumbled as it came to life, and she was pressed gently in her seat as it started to roll forward. Undoubtedly, she felt strange before, but at this moment, she could only feel a serene peace that she hadn't felt in forever. She truly was leaving everything behind, and it was for the best. From now on, she would only move forward and live in a way that her husband could be proud of.

Eventually, the plane's front wheels lifted off the Earth, and Valeria was sent toward the rest of her life.

IF YOU ENJOY PARANORMAL PSYCHICS, then check out Tasia Jackson in **Cold Read**.

Tasia is a psychic working occasional cases with the police department and the rare one-off for an old friend at the FBI. Her real business is super-secret because even the government doesn't know just how powerful and dangerous she is and what she can actually do. Her FBI friend Daniel Cordeiro probably has his suspicions, but he's never voiced them until she gets a strange vision of him pleading for her help.

Daniel's latest case is a run-of-the-mill missing persons, but it's personal this time. It's his missing person, his sister, and he's desperate to beat the 48-hour clock imposed by her kidnapper. So he goes it alone and gets himself in deep trouble. His hail-Mary hope is Tasia and the powers she is afraid to fully use. He can only pray she hears him when he calls...

Can Tasia tap into things she knows are better left alone in time to save innocent lives, or will her dangerous magic do them all more harm than good?

Book List

Tempest
  Half Demon
  Wanted Undead or Alive
  My Soul to Reap
  Gravetide
  Vance and Vance
  Cold Read
  Witch's Justice
  That's the Spirit
  Ancestor's Magic
  Strange Magic
  Magic Huntress
  Red Rising
  Relic Huntress
  Dead Wrong
  Her Dark Pleasure
  Blade of the Guild
  While You Were Reaping
  Thorne Sisters Chronicles

Possessed by Magic
Reincarnated by Magic
Immortal by Magic
Magic of the Night
Raven Magic

About the Author

Renee Joiner has been in love with the supernatural for longer than she can remember, so it is no surprise that she is an author of paranormal urban fantasy. Although she discovered her passion for writing when she was only twelve years old, she didn't make her writing debut until many years into the future. Adventurous and fun-loving, she enjoys traveling to new places, exploring new sights and meeting new people. Thus, she delights in creating fantastical worlds that are sure to give her readers an escape from the real world while simultaneously providing thrilling entertainment.

Besides her special knack for writing, you'll also find a passion for metaphysics spirituality which she has been nurturing for over four decades. Renee hails from New York and currently resides with her husband in their empty nest—unless you count their three adorable fur babies—in Florida. She enjoys adding to her sea of knowledge and thus spends her free time learning new things.

To find out more about Renee Joiner, feel free to visit her **official website**.

facebook.com/reneejoinerauthor

twitter.com/iamreneejoiner

instagram.com/reneejoinerauthor

amazon.com/author/reneejoiner

Thank you for reading my book!
I really appreciate all of your feedback and I love to hear what you have to say. Please leave your review at your favorite retailer!